Philip José Farmer was born in 1  University, he gained a BA in E shocked the SF world with the pu

sor of
d that
y the
n able
ple of
r and
linois.

By the same author

PHILIP JOSÉ FARMER

The Image of the Beast

An Exorcism: Ritual One

PANTHER
Granada Publishing

Panther Books
Granada Publishing Ltd
8 Grafton Street, London W1X 3LA

Published by Panther Books 1985

First published in Great Britain by
Quartet Books Limited 1975

Copyright © Philip José Farmer 1968

ISBN 0-586-06210-6

Reproduced, printed and bound in Great Britain by
Hazell Watson & Viney Limited,
Aylesbury, Bucks
Set in Baskerville

1

GREEN MILK CURDLED

Smoke rose to the light, and smoke and light fused to become green milk. The milk fissioned to become smoke and darkness above. As below.

Smog was outside, and smog was inside.

Green and sour.

The green and sour odour and taste came not only from the smog, which had forced its tendrils into the air-conditioned building, nor from the tobacco plumes in the room. It came from memory of what he had seen that morning and anticipation of what he would see within the next few minutes.

The film room of the Los Angeles Police Department was darker than Herald Childe had ever seen it. The beam of light from the projection booth usually tended to make grey what otherwise would have been black. But the cigar and cigarette smoke, the smog, and the mood of the viewers, blackened everything. Even the silver light from the screen seemed to pull light in instead of casting it back at the viewers.

Where the beam overhead struck the tobacco fumes, green milk formed and curdled and soured. So thought Herald Childe. The image was unforced. The worst smog in history was smothering Los Angeles and Orange counties. Not a mouse of a wind had stirred for a day and a night and a day and a night. On the third day, it seemed that this condition might go on and on.

The smog. He could now forget the smog.

Spread-eagled on the screen was his partner (possibly ex-partner). The wine-red draperies behind him glowed, and Matthew Colben's face, normally as red as Chianti half-diluted with water, was now the colour of a transparent plastic bag bulging with wine.

The camera swung away to show the rest of his body and some of the room. He was flat on his back and nude. His arms were strapped down beside him and his legs, also strapped down, formed a V. His penis lolled across his left thigh like a fat drunken worm.

The table must have been made for just this purpose of tying down men with their legs separated so others could walk in between the legs.

5

There was only the Y-shaped wooden table, the thick wine-red carpet, and the wine-red draperies. The camera swept around to show the circle of draperies and then turned back and swooped up to show the full form of Matthew Colben as seen by a fly on the ceiling. Colben's head was on a dark pillow. He looked straight up at the camera and smiled sillily. He did not seem to care that he was bound and helpless.

The previous scenes had shown why he did not care and had demonstrated how Colben had progressed, through conditioning, from impotent fear to rigid anticipation.

Childe, having seen the complete film once, felt his entrails slip about each other and knot each other and, their tails coiled around his backbone, pull until they were choking each other.

Colben grinned, and Childe murmured, 'You fool! You poor fucking fool!'

The man in the seat on Childe's right shifted and said, 'What'd you say?'

'Nothing, Commissioner.'

But his penis felt as if it were being sucked back up into his belly and drawing his testicles after it.

The draperies opened, and the camera moved in to show a huge black-rimmed, long-lashed, dark-blue eye. Then it moved down along a straight narrow nose and broad, full, and bright red lips. A pink-red tongue slipped out between unnaturally white and even teeth, shot back and forth a few times, dropped a bead of saliva on the chin, and then disappeared.

The camera moved back, the draperies were thrust open, and a woman entered. Her black glossy hair was combed straight back and fell to her waist. Her face was garish with beauty patches, rouge, powder, green and red and black and azure paint around the eyes and a curl of powder-blue down her cheeks, artificial eyelashes, and a tiny golden nose-ring. A green robe, tied at her neck and waist, was so thin that she might as well have been naked. Despite which she untied the cords about the neck and waist and slid the robe off and showed that she could be even more naked.

The camera moved downward and closer. The hollow at the base of the neck was deep and the bones beneath hinted at exquisiteness. The breasts were full but not large, slightly conical and up-tilted, with narrow and long, almost sharp, nipples. The breasts were hung upon a large rib cage. The belly sank inwards; she was skinny about

6

the hips, the bones stuck out just a little. The camera went round, or she pivoted – Childe could not tell which because the camera was so close to her and he had no reference point. Her buttocks were like huge unshelled soft-boiled eggs.

The camera travelled around her, showing the narrow waist and ovoid hips and then turned so that it was looking up towards the ceiling – which was covered with a drape-like material the colour of a broken blood-vessel in a drunkard's eye. The camera glanced up her white thigh; light was cast into the hollow between the legs – she must have spread her legs then – and there was the little brown eye of the anus and the edge of the mouth of her vagina. The hairs were yellow, which meant that the woman had either dyed her head hairs or her pubic hairs.

The camera, still pointing upwards, passed between her legs – which looked like the colossal limbs of a statue now – and then travelled slowly upward. It straightened out as it rose and was looking directly at her pubes. These were partly covered by a triangular cloth which was taped on. Childe did not know why. Modesty certainly was not the reason.

He had seen this shot before, but he braced himself. The first time, he – in common with the others in the room – had jumped and some had sworn and one had yelled.

The cloth was tight against the genitals, and a shift in angle of lighting suddenly revealed that the cloth was semi-transparent. The hairs formed a dark triangle, and the slit took in the cloth enough to show that the cloth was tight against the slit.

Abruptly, and Childe jumped again even though he knew what was coming, the cloth sank in more deeply, as if something inside the vagina had spread the lips open. Then something bulged against the cloth, something that could only have come from within the woman. It thrust the cloth up; the cloth shook as if a tiny fist or head were beating against it, and then the bulge sank back, and the cloth was quiet again.

The Commissioner, two seats away from Childe, said, 'What the hell could that be?' He blew out cigar smoke and then began coughing. Childe coughed, too.

'It could be something mechanical up her cunt,' Childe said. 'Or it could be . . .' He let the words, and his thoughts, hang. No hermaphrodite, as far as he knew, had a penis within the vaginal canal. Anyway, that wasn't a penis sliding out; that looked like an independent entity – gave the feeling of one, rather – and certainly the thing had beat against the cloth at more than one place.

Now the camera swung around at a level a few inches above Colben and several feet in front of him. It showed the feet, seemingly enormous at this narrow distance, the thickly muscled and hairy calves and thighs spread out on the Y-shaped table, the big testicles, the fat worm of the penis, no longer lolling against the thigh but beginning to get fatter and to lift its swollen red head. Colben could not have seen the woman enter, but he had evidently been conditioned so that he knew she would come in within a certain time after he was strapped to the table. The penis was coming to life as if its ears – buried within the flesh like a snake's – had heard her or as if the slit in its head were a detector of body heat – like an adder's nose pits – and it knew that she was in the room.

The camera moved to one side so that it could start with the profile of Matthew Colben's head. The thick curly grey-and-black hair, the big red ears, the smooth forehead, the big curved nose, the thin lips, massive jawbone, chin thick and heavy as the head of a sledge, big fat chest, the outcurve of a paunch grown with much stuffing of steak and beer, the down-curve to the penis, now fully up and swollen and hard. The camera moved in for a close shot; the veins were ropes run into the lanyard of lust (Childe could not help thinking in such images; he fingered concepts with a Midas touch). The head, fully exposed, glistened with lubricating fluid.

Now the camera moved up and away and took a position where both the man and woman could be seen. She approached slowly, swaying her hips, and came up to Colben and said something. Her lips moved, but there was no sound, and the police lip-reader could not tell what she was saying because her head was bent too far over. Colben said something too, but his words were undecipherable for the same reason.

The woman bent over and let her left breast fall so that Colben could take it in his mouth. He sucked for a while; and then the woman removed it. The camera moved in to show the nipple, which was wet and swollen. She kissed him on the mouth; the camera moved in sidewise to show her as she raised her head a little to permit the camera to record the tongue sliding back and forth into Colben's mouth. Then she began to kiss and to lick his chin, his neck, his chest, his nipples, and she smeared his round belly with saliva. She worked slowly down to his pubic hairs, slobbered on them, gently tapped his penis with her tongue many times, kissed it lightly several times, flicked out her tongue to dab its head with the tip while she held his penis at the root. Then she walked around the leg of the Y and between the legs and began to suck on his penis energetically.

At this point, a tinny piano, like those played in the old-time bars or in the silent movie theatres, began Dvořák's *Humoresque*. The camera shifted to a position above Colben's face; his eyes were closed and he was looking ecstatic, that is, stupidly happy.

For the first time, the woman spoke.

'Tell me just before you're ready to come, darling. Maybe thirty or so seconds before, yes? I have a beautiful surprise for you. Something new.'

The voice had been printed and run off by the police on an oscilloscope and studied. But distortions had been introduced into it. That was why the voice sounded so hollow and wavery.

'Go slower, baby,' Colben said. 'Take it easy, put it off like you did the last time. That was the greatest orgasm I ever had in my life. You're going a little too fast now. And don't stick your fingers up my ass like you did then. You cut my piles.'

The first time the scene had been shown, some of the cops had snickered. Nobody snickered now. There was an unheard but easily felt shift in the audience now. The smoke seemed to get hard and brittle; the green milk in the light beam became more sour. The Commissioner sucked in air so hard a rattle sounded in his throat and then he began coughing.

The piano was playing the *William Tell* overture now. The tinny music was so incongruous, and yet it was the incongruity that made it seem so horrible.

The woman raised her head and said, 'You about ready to come, *mon petit*?'

Colben breathed, 'Oh, Jesus, just about!'

The woman looked into the camera and smiled. The flesh seemed to fade away, the bones beneath were faintly glowing and cloudy. Then the flesh was cloudy; the skull was hard and bright. And then the skull faded and flesh fell back into place.

She leered into the camera and put her head down again, but this time she went past the corner of the Y and squatted down below the table, where the camera followed her. There was a small shelf fixed to one leg of the table. She picked something off it; the light brightened, the camera moved in nearer.

9

She held a pair of false teeth. They looked as if they were made of iron; the teeth were sharp as a razor and pointed like a tiger's.

She smiled and put the iron teeth on the shelf and used both hands to remove her own teeth. She looked thirty years older. She placed the white teeth on the shelf and then inserted the iron teeth into her mouth. She held the edge of her forefinger between the two teeth and bit gently down. Then she removed the finger and held it so that the camera could zero in on it. Bright red blood was welling out from the bite.

She stood up and wiped the cut on the fat glans of Colben's penis and she bent over and licked the blood off. Colben groaned and said, 'Oh, God. I'm going to come!'

Her mouth went around the head and she sucked in loudly. Colben began to jerk and to groan. The camera showed his face for a second before it moved back to a position alongside the woman's.

She raised her head quickly. The penis was jerking and spurting the thick oily whitish fluid. She opened her mouth widely, bent down swiftly and bit. The muscles along her jaw lumped; her neck muscles became cords.

Colben screamed

She whipped her head back and forth and bit again and again. Blood ran down from her mouth and reddened the pubic hairs.

The camera moved away from her to show the draperies through which she had entered. There was a flourish of trumpets. A cannon boomed in the distance. The piano played Tchaikovsky's *1812 Overture*.

Trumpets sounded again as the music faded. The draperies shot open, propelled by two stiff arms. A man stepped inside and posed for a moment, his right arm raised so that his black cloak half-hid his face. His hair was black and shiny as patent leather and was parted down the middle. His forehead and nose were white as the belly of a shark. His eyebrows were thick and black and met over his nose. The eyes were large and black.

He was dressed as if he were going to a movie premiere. He had on a formal suit, a stiff white shirt with a black formal tie and a diagonal red band across his chest and a medal or order on his lapel.

He wore blue sneakers.

Another comic element which only made the situation more horrible.

The man lowered the cloak to show a large hooked nose, a thick

10

black moustache which curved down around the ends of his thick rouged lips, and a prominent cleft chin.

He cackled, and this deliberately corny element was even more horrible than the sneakers. The laugh was a parody of all the gloating laughs cranked forth by all the monsters and Draculas of every horror movie.

Up went the arm, and, his face hidden behind the cloak, the man rushed towards the table. Colben was still screaming. The woman jumped away swiftly and let the man into the Y. The penis was still jerking and emitting blood and spermatic fluid; the head was half bitten off. The camera switched to the woman's face. Blood was running down her chin and over her breasts.

Again, the camera panned back to the Dracula (so Childe thought of him). Dracula cackled again, showing two obviously false canines, long and sharp. Then he bent down and began to chew savagely on the penis but within a short time raised his head. The blood and spermatic fluid was running out of his mouth and making the front of his white shirt crimson. He opened his mouth and spit out the head of the penis on to Colben's belly and laughed, spraying blood over himself and Colben.

The first time, Childe had fainted. This time, he got up and ran towards the door but vomited before he reached it. He was not alone.

2

The Dracula and the woman had looked into the camera and laughed wildly as if they had been having a hilarious time. Then, fade-out, and a flash of TO BE CONTINUED? End of film.

Herald Childe did not see the ending the second time. He was too occupied with groaning, with wiping the tears from his eyes and blowing his nose and coughing. The taste and odour of vomit were strong. He felt like apologizing, but he repressed the impulse. He had nothing to apologize for.

The Commissioner, who had not thrown up but who might have looked better if he had, said, 'Let's get out of here.'

He stepped over the mess on the wooden floor. Childe followed him. The others came out. The Commissioner said, 'We're going to have a conference, Childe. You can sit in on it, contribute if you wish.'

'I'd like to keep in touch with the police, Commissioner. But I don't have anything to contribute. Not just yet, anyway.'

He had told the police, more than once, everything he knew about Matthew Colben, which was much, and everything he knew about his disappearance, which was nothing.

The Commissioner was a tall lean man with a half-bald head and a long thin face and melancholy black moustache. He was always tugging at the right end of his moustache – never the left. Yet he was left-handed. Childe had observed this habit and wondered about its origin. What would the Commissioner say if he were made aware of it?

What could he say? Only he and a psychotherapist would ever be able to find out.

'You realize, Childe, that this comes at a very bad time for us,' the Commissioner said. 'If it weren't for the ... uh, extraordinary aspects of the case ... I wouldn't be able to spend more than a few minutes on it. As it is ...'

Childe nodded and said, 'Yes. I know. The Department will have to get on it later. I'm grateful that you've taken this time.'

'Oh, it's not that bad!' the Commissioner said. 'Sergeant Bruin will be handling the case. That is, when he has time. You have to realize ...'

'I realize,' Childe said. 'I know Bruin. I'll keep in touch with him. But not so often he'll be bugged.'

'Fine, fine!'

The Commissioner stuck out a skinny and cold, but sweating hand, and said, 'See you!' and turned and walked off down the hall.

Childe went into the nearest men's room, where several plain clothesmen and two uniformed men were washing the taste of vomit out. Sergeant Bruin was also there, but he had not been sick. He came from the stall zipping up his fly. Bruin was rightly named. He looked like a grizzly, but he was far less easily upset.

As he washed his hands, he said, 'I gotta hurry, Childe. The Commissioner wants a quick conference about your partner, and then we all gotta get back on this smog thing.'

'You have my phone number, and I got yours,' Childe said. He drank another cup of water and crumpled the paper and threw it into the wastepaper basket. 'Well, at least I'll be able to move around. I got a permit to use my car.'

'That's more'n several million citizens got right now,' Bruin said cheerfully. 'Be sure you burn the gas in a good cause.'

'So far, I haven't got much reason to burn anything,' Childe said. 'But I'm going to try.'

Bruin looked down at him. His big black eyes were as impenetrable as a bear's; they did not look human. He said, 'You going to put in time for free on this job?'

'Who's going to pay me?' Childe said. 'Colben's divorced. This case is tied up with Budler's, but Budler's wife discharged me yesterday. She says she doesn't give a shit any more.'

'He may be dead, just like Colben,' Bruin said. 'I wouldn't be surprised if we got another package through the mails.'

'Me neither,' Childe said.

'See you,' Bruin said. He put a heavy paw on Childe's shoulder for a second. 'Doing it for nothing, eh? He was your partner, right? But you was going to split up, right? Yet you're going to find out who killed him, right?'

'I'll try,' Childe said.

'I like that,' Bruin said. 'There ain't much sense of loyalty kicking around nowadays.' He lumbered off; the others trailed out after him. Childe was alone. He looked into the mirror over the washbowl. The pale face resembled Lord Byron's enough to have given him trouble with women – and a number of jealous or desirous men – ever since

13

he was fourteen. Now, it was a little lumpy, and a scar ran down his left cheek. Memento of Korea, when a drunken soldier had objected to being arrested by Childe and had slashed his face with the broken end of a beer bottle. The eyes were dark grey and just now much bloodshot. The neck below the slightly lumpy Byronic head was thick and the shoulders were wide. The face of a poet, he thought as he had thought many times, and the body of a cop, a private investigator. Why did you ever get into this sordid soul-leaching depressing corrupting racket? Why didn't you become a quiet professor of English or psychology in a quiet college town?

Only he and a psychotherapist would ever know, and he evidently did not want to know, since he had never gone to a psychotherapist. He was sure that he enjoyed the sordidness and tears and grief and hatred and the blood, somewhere in him. Something fed on contemptible food. Something enjoyed it, but that something sure as hell wasn't Herald Childe. Not at this moment, anyway.

He left the washroom and went down the hall to an elevator and dropped while he turned his thoughts so inwardly that he did not know whether or not he was alone in the cage. On the way to the exit, he shook his head a little as if to wake himself up. It was dangerous to be so infolded.

Matthew Colben, his partner, had been on his way to being his ex-partner. Colben was a big-mouthed braggart, a Don Juan who let his desire to make a pass interfere with his business. He had not allowed his prick to get in the way of business when he and Childe had become partners six years ago. But Colben was fifty now and perhaps trying to keep the thoughts of a slowing-down body and thickening flesh and a longer time to recover from hangovers away from him. Childe didn't accept this reason; Colben could do whatever he wanted after business hours, but he was cheating his partner when he cheated himself with the booze and the women. After the Budler case, they would be through. So Childe had promised himself.

Now Colben was dead and Budler could be in the hands of the same people who had taken Colben – although there was no evidence to indicate so. But Budler and Colben had disappeared the same night, and Colben had been tailing Budler.

The film had been mailed from a Torrance post office three days ago. Colben and Budler had been missing fourteen days.

Childe stopped at the tobacco stand and bought a morning *Times*. At any other time, the Colben case would have been headline

14

material. Not today. It was, however, a feature on the front page. Childe, hating to go outside, leaned against the wall and read the story. It had been considerably bowdlerized by the reporters who had seen the film. They had not been present at either of the showings he had witnessed, but Bruin had told him they were at a special running. Bruin had laughed like a bear with a sore throat, and described how at least half of them had thrown up or been close to throwing up.

'Some of them been in battles and seen men with their guts blowed inside out!' Bruin had said. 'You was in the Korean action and you was an officer, right? Yet you got sick! How come?'

'Didn't you feel your cock drawing up in your belly?' Childe had said.

'Naw.'

'Maybe you don't have one,' Childe had said. Bruin thought that was funny, too.

The whole story was in two columns, and it covered most of what Childe knew except for the details of the film. Colben's car had been found in a parking lot behind a trust and security building on Wilshire Boulevard in Beverly Hills. Colben had been trailing Benjamin Budler, a wealthy Beverly Hills lawyer. Budler had been stepping out on his wife, not to mention his regular mistress. The wife had hired *Childe & Colben, Private Investigators*, to get enough evidence for her to file for divorce.

Colben, using the tape recorder in his car, had described Budler's moves. Budler had picked up a lovely brunette (described in detail but unidentified) on the corner of Olympic and Veteran. The traffic light had been green, but Budler had held up a long line of cars, horns blaring, while he opened the door and let the woman in. She was well-dressed. Colben had surmised that her car was parked somewhere close; she did not look as if she would live in this neighbourhood.

Budler's Rolls-Royce had turned right on Veteran and gone to Santa Monica, where it had turned left and travelled down Santa Monica until it stopped a block from a quiet and expensive restaurant. Here Budler had let the woman off and driven to a parking place on a side street. He had walked to the restaurant where they had dined and wined (presumably) for three hours. Though they went in separately, they came out together. Budler was red-faced, talking loudly and laughed much. The woman laughed much also but she walked steadily. His balance was a little uncertain; he stumbled when he started across the street and almost fell.

They had taken the Rolls-Royce (with Budler driving too swiftly and weaving in and out of traffic) up Santa Monica and turned left at Bedford Drive to go north.

The tape was wiped clean from this point on.

Colben had stated that he had got some long-range pictures of the woman when Budler had picked her up. The camera was in the car but the film had been removed.

The car had been thoroughly cleaned; there was not a single fingerprint. Some dirt particles, presumably from the shoes of whoever had driven the car to the parking lot, were on the mat, but an analysis had shown only that the dirt could have come from anywhere in the area. There were some fibres; these had been rubbed off the rag used to wipe the seats.

Budler's Rolls-Royce was also missing.

The police had not discovered that Budler had dropped out of his normal pattern of life until two days after Colben was reported missing. His wife had known that he was gone, but she had not bothered to report this. Why should she? He often did not come home for two to four days.

As soon as she was informed that her husband might have been kidnapped or murdered, that his disappearance was connected with that of Colben (or seemed likely to be connected), she had told Childe that he was no longer employed by her.

'I hope they find the son of a bitch dead! And soon!' she had screamed over the phone. 'I don't want his money tied up forever! I need it now! It's just like him to never be found and tie me up with litigation and red tape and all that shit! Just like him! I hate him!' and so on.

'I'll send you my bill,' Childe had replied. 'It was nice to be able to work for you,' and he had hung up.

His bill would be delivered, but how soon he would be paid was doubtful. Even if a cheque was sent by Mrs Budler by return mail, it might not be cashable for some time. The newspapers reported that the authorities were discussing closing down all banks until the crisis was over. Many people were protesting against this, but it would not make much difference for the protesters if the banks did stay open. What good did that do if most of the customers could not get to their bank unless they were within walking distance or wanted to stand in line for hours to take the infrequent bus?

He looked up from the paper. Two uniformed, gas-masked men were bringing in a tall dark man between them. He held up handcuffed hands as if to demonstrate his martyrdom to the world. One cop carried a third gas mask, and by this Childe knew that the arrested man had probably been using a mask while holding up a store or robbing a loan company or doing something which required concealing his face.

Childe wondered why the cops were bringing him in through this entrance. Perhaps they had caught him just down the street and were taking the short cut.

The situation was advantageous for criminals in one respect. Men wearing gas masks or water-soaked cloths over their faces were not uncommon. On the other hand, anyone abroad was likely to be stopped and questioned. One thing balances out another.

The cops and the arrestee were coughing. The man behind the tobacco counter was coughing. Childe felt a tickling in his throat. He could not smell the smog, but the thought of smelling it evoked the ghost of a cough.

He checked his ID cards and permit. He did not want to be caught without them, as he had been yesterday. He had lost about an hour because, even after the cops had called in and validated his reasons for being out, he had been required to go home and pick up his papers, and he had been stopped again before he could get home.

He tucked the paper under his arm, walked to the door, looked through the glass, shuddered, wished he had a lightweight scuba diver's equipment, opened the door and plunged in.

3

It was like walking at the bottom of a sea of very thin bile.

There were no clouds between the sun and the sea. The sun shone brightly as if it were trying to burn a path through the sea. The August sun burned fiercely and the more it burned, the more it cut with its yellow machetes, the thicker and more poisonous grew the grey-green foliage.

(Childe knew he was mixing metaphors. So what? The Cosmos was a mixed metaphor in the mind of God. The left mind of God did not know what the right mind of God was doing. Or did not care. God was a schizophrenic? Herald Childe, creature of God, image of God, certainly was schizophrenic, Levorotatory image?)

Eyes burned like heretics at the stake. Sinuses were scourged; fire ran along the delicate bones; spermaticky fluid collected to fill the chambers of the sinuses and dripped, waiting for the explosion of air voluntarily or involuntarily set off, to discharge the stuff with the mildest of orgasms.

Not a twitch of wind. The air had been unmoving for a day and a night and half a day, as if the atmosphere had died and was rotting.

The grey-green stuff hung in sheets. Or seemed to. The book of judgement was being read and the pages, the grey-green sheets, were being turned as the eye read and more and more pages were being piled towards the front of the book. How far to read before the end?

Childe could see no farther than one hundred and ten feet, if that. He had walked this path from the door to the parking lot so many times that he could not get lost. But there were those who did not know where they were. A woman, screaming, ran by him, and was lost in the greenishness. He stopped. His heart was pounding. Faintly, he could hear a car horn. A siren wailed somewhere. He turned slowly, trying to see or hear the woman or her pursuer, if any, but there was nothing. She ran; no one pursued.

He began to trot. He sweated. His eyes smarted and flowed tears, and little flames seemed to be creeping down his throat towards his lungs. He wanted to get to the car, which held his gas mask. He forced himself to walk. There was panic hanging in the air, the same panic that came to a man when he felt hands squeezing his neck and thumbs pressing in on his windpipe.

A car emerged from the cloud. It was not his. He passed by it and, ten parking spaces on, found his 1970 Oldsmobile. He put the mask on, started the motor, wincing a little at the thought of the poisons shooting out of the exhaust, turned his lights on and drove out of the lot. The street held more moving bright lights than he had expected. He turned on the radio and found out why. Those who had some place to go outside the area of smog were going whether or not the authorities gave permission, and so the authorities were giving permission. Many who had no place to go, but were going anyway, were also driving out. The flood had started. The streets weren't jammed as yet, but they soon would be.

Childe cursed. He had planned on easy drives to his various destinations that day because, although he could not drive swiftly, he could drive unimpeded by traffic.

The voice of the governor issued from the speaker. The governor pleaded for restraint and calm. Everybody should continue to stay home – if they were able to do so. However, those who had to get out for health reasons (which would include the entire population now, Childe thought) should drive carefully and should realize that there just were not enough accommodations for them outside the Los Angeles–Orange County area in this state. Nevada and Arizona had been notified of the invasion, and Utah and New Mexico were readying themselves. Troops were being moved into the area but only to act as traffic policemen and to assist the hospitals. There was no martial law; there was no need for it. There was an upswing in crimes of passion, theft, and robbery, but there had been no riots.

No wonder, thought Childe. There was something irritating about smog; it did eat the skin off the nerves, but people did not like to get out in it, and people did not collect in large numbers. To every man, others looked like ghosts coming towards him out of the grey-greenness or like strange fish appearing suddenly from the shadows. Strange fish could be sharks.

He passed a car with three goggled, snouted monstrosities in it. Their heads swivelled, the cyclopean eyes stared blindly, the noses seemed to sniff. He sped away from them until their headlights were muffled and then slowed down. Once, a car suddenly appeared behind him, and a red light flashed. He looked through the rear view mirror before he stopped; there were fake prowl cars stopping motorists and robbing, beating, or even killing them on the streets during daylight, within twenty feet of passers-by. He decided to pull over, eased the car gently towards the dimly visible kerb, and stopped. He kept the motor running and peered at the car and the cop getting out of it on the right side. If he did not like the looks of them he could still get out of the right side of his car and take off into the dimness. But he recognized the cop, although he did not know his name, and stayed behind the wheel. He flipped open his coat and slowly reached within it so that the cop would not get the impression he was reaching for a gun. He had a licence for a gun but it was at home.

The cops had stopped too many to make him get out of the car and assume the stance of the friskee. Besides, there were many legitimate drivers, and within a short time, there would be so many cars on the streets that they might as well give up, except for obvious cases.

Childe established his identity quickly enough. They knew him by hearsay and had also read the papers. One, Chominshi, wanted to discuss the case, but the other was coughing, and Childe started to cough, so they let him go. He continued up Third towards West Los Angeles. His apartment and his office were a few blocks away from Beverly Hills. He planned to go straight home and do some thinking.

If he could think. He was in a mild state of shock. His reflexes seemed to be slow, as if he had been drugged or was recovering from being knocked out. He felt a slight sense of detachment, as if he had been disengaged somewhat from reality, no doubt to soften the effects of the film. The smog did not help him keep an anchor on things; it induced a feeling of slippage of self.

He was not burning with lust for revenge on those who had killed Colben. He had not liked Colben, and he knew that Colben had done some things which were criminal but he had escaped without (as far as Childe knew) even the punishment of conscience. He had knocked up a teenager and kicked her out, and the girl had taken sleeping pills and died. There were others, although none had ended in death for the girls. But some would have been better off dead. And there was the wife of a client who had been found beaten and would always be an idiot. Childe had had no basis for suspicion of Colben, but he had felt that Colben might have done the beating for the client, especially after he had discovered that Colben was going to bed with the woman. He could prove nothing; he could not even make an accusation which would not sound stupid, because he lacked any evidence. That Colben was neglecting the business, however, was reason enough to get rid of him. Childe did not have enough money to buy Colben out; he had meant to make it so unpleasant for Colben that he would be glad to dissolve the partnership.

Nevertheless, no man deserved to die as Colben had. Or did he? The horror was more in the viewers' minds than in Colben's. He had been hurt very much, but only briefly, and had died quickly.

That did not matter. Childe intended to find out all he could, although he suspected that he would find out very little. And soon enough the need to pay bills would take him off the case; he would only be able to work on it during his leisure moments. Which meant that, in effect, he would be able to accomplish almost nothing.

But he had nothing else to do, and he certainly did not intend to sit still in his apartment and breathe in poison gas. He had to do something to keep going. He could not even read comfortably because of the burning and the tears. He was like a shark that has to keep moving to allow water to flow through the gills. Once he stopped, he would suffocate.

But a shark can breathe and also stand still if the water is moving. Sybil could be his flowingness. Sybil was a name that sounded like running brooks and sunshine in quiet green glades and wisdom like milk from full flowing breasts. Certainly not green milk. White creamy milk of tenderness and good sense.

Childe smiled. The Great Romanticist. He not only looked like Lord Byron, he thought like him. Reincarnation come. George Gordon, Lord Byron, reborn as a private eye and without a club foot. One thing about a club mind, it didn't show. Not at first. But the limp became evident to others who had to walk with him day after day.

The Private Eyes of the novels. They were simple straightforward men with their minds made up – all black and white – vengeance is mine, saith Lord Hammer – true heroes with whom the big majority of readers had no trouble identifying.

This was strange, because the antiheroes of the existential novels were supposed to be representative of the modern mind, and they certainly were uncertain. The antihero got far more publicity, far more critical trumpeting, than the simple, stable, undoubting private eye, the hero of the masses.

Childe told himself to cut, as if his thoughts were a strip of film. He was exaggerating and also simplifying. Inwardly, he might be an existential antihero, but outwardly he was a man of action, a Shadow, a Doc Savage, a Sam Spade. He smiled again. Truth to tell, he was Herald Sigurd Childe, red-eyed, watery-eyed, drippy-nosed, sickened, wanting to run home to Mother. Or to that image named Sybil.

Mother, unfortunately, became angry if he did not phone her to ask if he could come over. Mother wanted privacy and independence, and if she did not get it, she expressed herself unpleasantly and exiled him for an indeterminate time.

He parked the car outside his apartment, ran up the steps, hearing someone cough behind a door as he passed, and unlocked his door. The apartment was a living room, a kitchenette, and a bedroom. Normally, it was bright with white walls and ceilings and creamy woodwork and lightly coloured, lightly built furniture. Today, it was gloomy; even the unshadowed places had a greenish tinge.

Sybil answered the phone before the second ring had started.

'You must have been expecting me,' he said gaily.

'I was expecting,' she said. Her voice was not, however, unfriendly.

He did not make the obvious reply. 'I'd like to come over,' he finally said.

'Why? Because you're hard up?'

'For your company.'

'You haven't got anything to do. You have to find some way to spend the time.'

'I have a case I'm working on,' he said. He hesitated and then, knowing that he was baiting the hook and hating himself for it, said, 'It's about Colben. You read the papers?'

'I thought that was what you'd be working on. Isn't it horrible?'

He did not ask her why she was home today. She was the secretary of an advertising agency executive. Neither she nor her boss would have a driving priority.

'I'll be right over,' he said. He paused and then said, 'Will I be able to stay a while or will I have to get out after a while? Don't get mad! I just want to know; I'd like to be able to relax.'

'You can stay for a couple of hours or more, if you like. I'm not going anyplace, and nobody is coming – that I know of.'

He took the phone from his ear but her voice was not loud enough for him to hear, and he returned it to his ear. 'Herald? I really do want you to come!'

He said, 'Good!' and then, 'Hell! I've just been thinking of myself! Is there anything I can get you from the store?'

'No, you know there's a supermarket only three blocks from here. I walked.'

'OK. I just thought you might not have gone out yet or you forgot something you might want me to pick up for you.'

They were both silent for a few seconds. He was thinking about his irritations when they had been married, about how many times he had had to run out to get things that she had forgotten during her shopping. She must be thinking about his recriminations, too; she was always thinking about them when they got together.

'I'll be right over,' he said hurriedly. 'So long.'

He hung up and left the apartment. The man was still coughing behind the door. A stereo suddenly blared Strauss' *Thus Spake Zarathustra* downstairs. Somebody protested feebly; the music continued to play loudly. The protests became louder, and there was a pounding on a wall. The music did not soften.

Herald considered walking the four blocks to Sybil's and then decided against it. He might need to take off suddenly, although there did not seem much chance of it. His answering service was not operating; it had no priority. He did not intend to leave Sybil's number with the police operator or Sergeant Bruin while he was with her. She would get unreasonably angry about this. She did not like to be interrupted by calls while she was with him, at least, not by business calls. That had been one of the things bugging her when they were man and wife. Theoretically, she should not be bothered by such matters now. In practice, which operates more on emotion than logic, she was as enraged as ever. He well knew how enraged. The last time he had been at her apartment, the exchange had interrupted them at a crucial moment, and she had run him out. Since then, he had called several times but had been cooled off. The last time he'd phoned had been two weeks ago.

She was right in one guess. He was hard up. But he did not expect to be any less so after seeing her. He intended to talk, to talk only, to soothe some troublings and to scare away the loneliness that had come more strongly after seeing the film of Colben.

It was strange, or, if not so strange, indicative. He had lived twenty of his thirty-five years in Los Angeles County. Yet he knew only one woman to whom he could really unburden himself and feel relaxed and certain of complete understanding. No. He was wrong. There was not even one woman, because Sybil did not completely understand him, that is, sympathize with him. If she did, she would not now be his ex-wife.

23

But Sybil had said the same thing about men in general and about him in particular. It was *the human situation* - whatever that phrase meant.

He parked the car in front of her apartment - no trouble finding parking space now - and went into the little lobby. He rang her bell; she buzzed; he went up the steps through the inner door and down the hall to the end. Her door was on the right. He knocked; the door swung open. Sybil was dressed in a floor-length morning robe with large red and black diamond shapes. The black diamonds contained a white ankh, the looped cross of the ancient Egyptians. Her feet were bare.

Sybil was thirty-four and five feet five inches tall. She had long black hair, sharp black eyebrows, large greenish eyes, a slender straight nose perhaps a little bit too long, a full mouth, a pale skin. She was pretty, and the body under the kimono was well built, although she may have been just a little too hippy for some tastes.

Her apartment was light, like his, with much white on the walls and ceilings, and creamy woodwork and light and airy furniture. But a tall gloomy El Greco reproduction hung incongruously on the wall; it hovered over everything said and done in the one room. Childe always felt as if the elongated man on the cross was delivering judgement upon him as well as upon the city on the plain.

The painting was not as visible as usual. There was almost always a blue haze of tobacco - which accounted for the walls and ceiling not being as white as those of his apartment - and today the blue had become grey-green. Sybil coughed as she lit another cigarette, and then she went into a spasm of coughing and her face became blue. He was not upset by this, no more than usual, anyway. She had incipient emphysema and had been advised by her doctor to chop off the smoking two years ago. Certainly, the smog was accelerating her disease, but he could do nothing about it. Still, it was one more cause for quarrelling.

She finally went into the kitchen for water and came out several minutes later. Her expression was challenging, but he kept his face smooth. He waited until she sat down on the sofa across the room from his easy chair. She ground the freshly lit cigarette out on an ash tray and said, 'Oh, God! I can't breathe!'

By which she meant that she could not smoke.

'Tell me about Colben,' she said, and then, 'first, could I get you . . ?'

24

Her voice decayed. She was always forgetting that he had quit drinking four years ago.

'I need to relax,' he said. 'I'm all out of pot and no chance to get any. You ..?'

'I'll get some,' she said eagerly. She rose and went into the kitchen. A panel creaked as it slid back; a minute passed; she came back with two cigarettes of white paper twisted at both ends. She handed him one. He said, 'Thanks,' and sniffed it. The odour always brought visions of flat-topped pyramids, of Aztec priests with sharp obsidian knives, naked brown men and women working in red clay fields under a sun fiercer than an eagle's glare, or Arab feluccas scudding along in the Indian Ocean. Why, he did not know.

He lit up and sucked in the heavy smoke and held it in his lungs as long as he could. He tried at the same time to empty his mind and body of the horror of this morning and the irritations he had felt since calling Sybil. There was no use smoking if he retained the bad feelings. He had to pour them out, and he could do it – sometimes. The discipline of meditation that a friend had taught him – or tried to teach him – had sometimes been effective. But he was a detective, and the prosecution of human beings, the tracking down, the immersion in hate and misery, negated the ability to meditate. Nevertheless, stubborn, he had persisted in trying, and he could sometimes empty himself. Or seem to. His friend said that he was not truly meditating; he was using a trick, a technique without essence.

Sybil, knowing what he was doing, said nothing. A clock ticked. A horn sounded faintly; a siren wailed. Sirens were always wailing nowadays. Then he breathed out and sucked in again and held his breath, and presently the *crystallization* came. There was a definite shifting of invisible lines, as if the currents of force that thread every centimetre of the universe had rearranged themselves into another *straighter* configuration.

He looked at Sybil and now he loved her very much, as he had loved her when they were first married. The snarls and knots were yanked loose; they were in a beautiful web which vibrated love and harmony through them with every movement they made. Never mind the inevitable spider.

4

He had hesitated to stop her when she kissed him all over his belly, although he knew what was coming. He continued to restrain himself when she took his penis and bent down to place her mouth around the head. He felt the tongue flicking it, shuddered, pushed her head away, though gently, and said, 'No!'

She looked up at him and said, 'Why?'

'I never got around to telling you the fine details of the film,' he said.

'You're getting soft!'

She sat up in the bed and looked down at him. She was frowning. 'Have you got a disease?'

'For God's sake!' he said, and he sat up, too. 'Do you think I'd go to bed with you if I knew I had the syph or the clap? What kind of a question – what kind of a person do you think I am?'

'I'm sorry,' she said. 'My God! What's wrong? What did I do?'

'Nothing. Nothing under most circumstances. But I felt as if my cock was frozen when you . . . Never mind. Let me explain why I couldn't let you go down on me.'

'I wish you wouldn't use words like that!'

'OK, my thing, then! Let me tell you.'

She listened with wide eyes. She was leaning on one arm near him. He could see the swollen nipple, which did not seem to dwindle a bit as she listened. It might have increased. Certainly, her eyes were bright, and, despite her expressed horror, she smiled now and then.

'I really think you'd like to do that to me!' he said.

'You're always saying something stupid like that,' she said. 'Even now. Do you hate me so much you can't even get a hard-on.'

'You mean erection, don't you?' he said. 'If you can't understand why my penis wanted to crawl into my belly for safety, then you can't understand anything about men.'

'I won't bite,' she said, and she grabbed his penis and lunged for it with her mouth wide open and smiling to show all her teeth.

He jerked himself away, saying, 'Don't!'

'Forget about it, I was just kidding you,' she said, and she crawled on to him and began kissing him. She thrust her tongue along his tongue and down his throat so far that he choked. 'For God's sake!'

he said, turning his head away. 'What the hell are you trying to do? I can't breathe!'

She sat up and almost hissed at him. 'You can't breathe! How do you think I breathe when you're shoving that big thing down my throat? What is the *matter*?'

'I don't know,' he said. He sat up. 'Let's have a few more drags. Maybe things'll straighten out.'

'Do you have to depend upon that to be able to love me?'

He tried to take her hand in his but she snatched it away.

'You didn't see it,' he said. 'Those iron teeth! The blood! Spitting out that bloody flesh! God!'

'I feel sorry for Colben,' she said, 'but I don't see what he has to do with us. You never liked him; you were going to get rid of him. And he gave me the creeps. Anyway . . . oh, I don't know.'

She rolled off the bed, went to the closet, and put on the kimono. She lit a cigarette and at once began coughing. It sounded as if her lungs were full of snot.

He felt angry, and opened his mouth to say something – what, he did not know, just so it was something that would hurt. But the taste of cunt made him pause. She had a beautiful cunt, the hair was thick and almost blue-black and so soft it felt almost like a seal pelt. She lubricated freely, perhaps too much, but the oil was sweet and clean. And she could squeeze down on his cock as if she had a hand inside it. And then he remembered the thing bulging out the pad over the woman's cunt in the film, and the blood that had been pouring into his penis became slushy and slowly thawed out and drained back into his body.

Sybil, who had seen the dawning erection, said, 'What's wrong *now*?'

'Sybil, there's nothing wrong with *you*. It's me. I'm too upset.'

She sucked in some more smoke and managed to check a cough.

'You always did bring your work home. No wonder our life became such a hell.'

He knew that that was not true. They had rubbed each other raw for other reasons, the causes of most of which they did not understand. There was, however, no use arguing. He had had enough of that.

He sat up and swung his legs over the bed and stood up and walked to the chair on which he had piled his clothes.

'What are you doing?'

'Some of the smog got in your brain?' he said. 'It's obvious I'm going to dress, and it's fairly predictable that I'm getting out of here.'

He checked the impulse to say, 'Forever!' It sounded so childish. But it could be true.

She said nothing. She swayed back and forth with her eyes closed for a minute, then, after opening them, spun around and walked into the living room. A minute later, he followed her. She was on the divan and glaring at him.

'I haven't had such a ball ache since I was a teenager and came home from my first necking party,' he said. He did not know why he said it; certainly, he did not expect her to feel sorry for him and to do something about it. Or did he?

'Necking party? You're sure dating yourself, old man!'

She looked furious. Unfortunately, fury did not make her beautiful.

Yet, he hated to leave; he had a vague feeling that he was somehow at fault.

He took one step towards her and stopped. He was going to kiss her, but it was force of habit that pushed him.

'Good-bye,' he said. 'I really am sorry, in a way.'

'In a way!' she screamed. 'Now isn't that just like you! You can't be all sorry or all righteously indignant or all right or all wrong! You have to be half-sorry. You . . . you . . . half-assed half-man!'

'And so we leave exotic Sybil-land,' he said, as he swung the door open. 'It sinks slowly into the smog of fantastic Southern California, and we say aloha, farewell, adieu, and kiss my ass!'

. Sybil sprang out of the chair with a scream and came at him with fingers hooked to catch his face with her nails. He caught them and shoved her back so that she staggered against the sofa. She caught herself and then yelled, 'You asshole! I hate you! I had a choice to make! I let you come here, instead of Al! I wanted you, not him! He was strictly second-choice, and a bad second at that! You think you're hard up, you don't know what hard up is! I've turned down lots of men because I kept hoping every night you'd call me! I'd eat you up; you'd be days getting out of here. I'd love you, oh, how I'd love you! And now this, you stinking bastard! Well, I'm going to call Al, and he's going to get everything I was going to give you and more! More! More! Do you understand that, you?'

He understood that he could still feel jealous. He felt like punching her and then waiting for Al and kicking him downstairs.

But it would be no good trying to make up with her. Not now. Actually, not ever, but he wasn't quite ready to believe this. Not down there where certainty dwelt.

Trying to grasp what ruined their love was like trying to close your fingers on a handful of smog.

He strode through the door and, knowing that she expected him to slam it behind him, did not.

Perhaps it was this that drove her to the last barbarism.

She stepped into the hall and shouted, 'I'll suck his cock! I'll suck his cock, you!'

He turned and shouted, 'You're no lady!' and spun around and walked off.

Outside, in the biting veils of grey-green, he laughed until he coughed raspingly, and then he cried. Part of the tears was engendered by the smog, part of his grief and rage. It was sad and heart-rending and disgusting and comical. One-upmanship was all right, but the one-upman actually upped it up his own one.

'When the hell is she going to grow up?' he groaned, and then. 'When the hell am *I*? When will the Childe become father to the man?'

Dante was thirty-five, midway in his life's journey, when he went astray from the straight road and woke to find himself alone in a dark wood.

But he obtained a professional guide, and he had at least once been on the straight road, the True Way.

Childe did not remember having been on the straight road. And where was his Virgil? The son of a bitch must be striking for higher pay and shorter hours.

Every man his own Virgil, Childe said, and coughing (like Miniver Cheevy), pushed through the smog.

5

Somebody had broken the left front window of the Olds while he was with Sybil. A glance at the front seat showed him why. The gas mask was gone. He cursed. The mask had cost him fifty dollars when he purchased it yesterday, and there were no more to be had except in the black market. The masks were selling for two hundred or more dollars, and it took time to locate a seller.

He had the time, but he did not have cash in hand and he doubted that his cheque would be accepted. The banks were closed, and the smog might disappear so suddenly that he would not need the mask and would stop payment of the cheque. There was nothing to do except use a wet handkerchief and a pair of goggles he had worn when he had a motorcycle. That meant he must return to his apartment.

He made up a pile of handkerchiefs and filled a canteen with water as soon as he was home. He dialled the LAPD to report the theft, but, after two minutes, he gave up. The line was likely to be busy all day and all night and indefinitely into the future. He brushed his teeth and washed his face. The wash rag looked yellow. Probably it was his imagination, but the yellow could be the smog coming out. The yellow looked like the stuff that clouded his windshield in the morning after several days of heavy smog. The air of Los Angeles was an ocean in which poisonous plankton drifted.

He ate a sandwich of cold sliced beef with dill pickles and drank a glass of milk, although he did not feel hungry. Visualizations of Sybil with Al troubled him. He didn't know Al, but he could not bar shadowy images whose only bright features – too bright – were a rigid monstrosity and a pair of hairy, never-empty testicles. The pump-pump-pumping sound was also only a shadow, but it would not go away either. Shadows sometimes turned out to be indelible ink blots.

He forced himself to consider Matthew Colben and his murderers. At least, he *thought* they were murderers. There was no proof that Colben had been killed. He might be alive, though not well, somewhere in this area. Or someplace else.

Now that he was recovering from his shock, he could even think that Colben might be untouched and the film faked.

He could think this, but he did not believe it.

The phone rang. Someone was getting through to him, even if he could get through to no one. Suspecting that only the police could ram through a call, he picked up the phone. Sergeant Bruin's voice, husky and growling like a bear just waking up from hibernation, said, 'Childe?'

'Yes.'

'We got proof that they mean business. That film wasn't faked.'

Childe was startled. He said, 'I was just thinking about a fraud. How'd you find out?'

'We just opened a package mailed from Pasadena.'

Bruin paused. Childe said, 'Yeah?'

'Yeah. Colben's prick was in it. The end of it, anyway. Somebody's prick, anyway. It sure as hell had been bitten off.'

'No leads yet?' Childe said after three seconds' hesitation.

'The package's being checked, but we don't expect anything, naturally. And I got bad news. I'm being taken off this case, well, almost entirely taken off. We got too many other things just now, you know why. If there's going to be any work done on this, Childe, you'll have to do it. But don't go off half-cocked and don't do nothing if you get a definite lead, which I think you ain't going to get. You know what I mean. You been in the business.'

'Yes, I know,' Childe said. 'I'm going to do what I can, which, as you said, probably won't be much. I have nothing else to do now, anyway.'

'You could come down here and swear in,' Bruin said. 'We need men right now! The traffic all over the city is a mess, like I never saw before. Everybody's trying to get out. This is going to be a ghost town. But it'll be a mess, a bloody mess, today and tomorrow. I'm telling you, I never seen nothing like it before.'

Bruin could be stolid about Colben, but the prospect of the greatest traffic jam ever unfroze his bowels. He was really being moved.

'If I need help, or if I stumble – and I mean stumble – across anything significant, should I call you?'

'You can leave a message. I'll call you back when – if – I get in. Good luck, Childe.'

'Same to you, Bruin,' Childe said and muttered as he hung up, '*O Ursus Horribilis!* Or whatever the vocative case is.'

He became aware that he was sweating, that his eyes felt as if they'd been filed, his sinuses hurt, he had a headache, his throat felt raw, his lungs were wheezing for the first time in five years since he had quit smoking tobacco, and, not too far off, horns were blaring.

He could do something to ease the effects of the poisoned air, but he could do little about the cars out in the street. When he had left his wife's apartment, he had had a surprising amount of trouble getting across Burton Way to San Vicente. There was no stop light at this point on Le Doux. Cars had to buck traffic coming down Burton Way on one side and going up on the other side of the divider. Coming down to the apartment, he had not seen a car or even a pair of headlights in the dimness. But, going back, he had had to be careful in crossing. The lights sprang out of the grey-greenness with startling rapidity as they rounded a nearby curve of Burton Way to the west. He had managed to find a break large enough to justify gunning across. Even so, a pair of lights and a blaring horn and squealing brakes and a shouted curse – subject to the Doppler effect – told him that a speeder had come close.

The traffic going west towards Beverly Hills was light, but that coming across Burton Way between the boulevards to cut southeast on San Vicente was heavy. There was panic among the drivers. The cars were two deep, then suddenly three deep, and Childe had barely had room to squeeze through. He was being forced out of his own lane and against the kerb. Several times, he only got by by rubbing his tyres hard against the kerb.

The light at San Vicente and Third was red for him, but the cars coming down San Vicente were going through it. A car going east on Third, horn bellowing, tried to bull its way through. It collided lightly with another. From what Childe could see, the only damage was crumpled fenders. But the two drivers, hopping out and swinging at each other, looked as if they might draw some blood, inept as they were with their fists. He had caught a glimpse of several frightened faces – children – looking through the windows of both damaged cars. Then he was gone.

Now he could hear the steady honking of horns. The great herd was migrating, and God help them.

The deadly stink and blinding smoke had been bad enough when most cars suddenly ceased operating. But now that two million automobiles were suddenly on the march, the smog was going to be intensified. It was true that, in time, the cars would be gone, and then the atmosphere could be expected to start cleaning itself. If it was going to do it. Childe had the feeling that the smog wasn't going to leave, although he knew that that was irrational.

Meanwhile, he, Childe, was staying. He had work to do. But would he be able to do anything? He had to get around, and it looked as if he might not be able to do that.

He sat down on the sofa, and looked across the room at the dark golden bookcases. *The Annotated Sherlock Holmes*, the two great boxed volumes, was his treasure, the culminating work of his collection unless you counted a copy of *The White Company* personally inscribed by A. Conan Doyle, once the possession of Childe's father. It was his father who had introduced him at an early age to interesting and stimulating books, and his father who had managed to pass on his devotion to the greatest detective to his son. But his father had remained a professor of mathematics; he had felt no burning to emulate The Master.

Nor would any 'normal' child. Most kids wanted to be aeroplane pilots or railroad engineers or cowboys or astronauts when they grew up. Many, of course, wanted to be detectives, Sherlock Holmeses, Mark Tidds (what boy nowadays knew of Mark Tidd?), even Nick Carters since he had been revived with modern settings and plots, but few stuck to that wish. Most of the policemen and private investigators whom he knew had not had these professions as boyhood goals. Many had never read Holmes or had done so without enthusiasm; he had never met a Holmes buff among them. But they did read true detective magazines and devoured the countless paperbacks of murder mysteries and of private eyes. They made fun of the books, but, like cowboys who also deride the genuineness of Westerns, they were addicted.

Childe made no secret of his 'vice'. He loved them, even the bad ones, and gloried in the 'good' ones.

And so why was he trying to justify being a detective? Was it something to be ashamed of?

In one way, it was. There was in every American, even the judge and the policeman, a more-or-less strong contempt for lawmen. This lived side by side with an admiration for the lawman, but for the lawman who is a strong individualist, who fights most of his battles by himself against overwhelming evil, who fights often outside the law in order to bring about justice. In short, the frontier marshal, the Mike Hammerish private eye. This lawman is so close to the criminal that there is a certain sympathy between the lawman and the criminal.

Or so it seemed to Childe, who, as he told himself now, tended to do too much theorizing and also to project his own feelings as those of others.

Matthew Colben. Where was he now? Dead or suffering? Who had forcibly taken him to some dwelling somewhere in this area? Why was the film sent to the LAPD? Why this gesture of mockery and defiance? What could the criminals hope to gain by it, except a perverse pleasure in frustrating the police?

There were no clues, no leads, except the vampire motif, which was nothing but a suggestion of a direction to take. But it was the only handle to grasp, ectoplasmic though it was, and he would try to seize it. At least, it would give him something to do.

He knew something about vampires. He had seen the early Dracula movies and the later movies on TV. Ten years ago, he had read the novel, *Dracula*, and found it surprisingly powerful and vivid and convincing. It was far better than the best Dracula movie, the first; the makers of the movie should have followed the book more closely. He had also read Montague Summers and had been an avid reader of the now-dead *Weird Tales* magazine. But a little knowledge was not dangerous; it was just useless.

There was one man he knew who was deeply interested in the occult and the supernatural. He looked up the number in his record book because it was unlisted and he had not called enough to memorize it. There was no response for about fifty seconds. He waited and then a recording informed him that he would soon be taken care of if he were patient but please not to use the phone unless it was an emergency. He hung up and turned on the radio. There was some news about the international and national situations, but most of the broadcast was about the exodus. A number of stalled cars on the freeways and highways had backed up traffic for a total of several thousand miles. The police were trying to restrict passage on the freeways to a certain number of lanes to permit the police cars, ambulances, and tow trucks to pass through. But all lanes were being used, and the police were having a hell of a time clearing them out. A number of fires had started in homes and buildings, and some of them were burning down with no assistance from the firemen because the trucks could not get through. There were collisions all over the area with no help available, not only because of the traffic but because there just was not enough hospital and police personnel available.

Childe thought, to hell with the case! I'll help!

He called the LAPD and hung on for fifteen minutes, but he got only a busy signal. He then called the Beverly Hills Police Department and got the same result. He had no more luck with the

Mount Sinai Hospital on Beverly Boulevard, which was within walking distance. He put drops in his eyes and snuffed up nose drops. He wet a handkerchief to place over his nose and put his goggles on top of his head. He stuck a pencil flashlight in one pocket and switch-blade knife in another. Then he left the apartment building and walked down San Vicente to Beverly Boulevard.

In the half hour that he had been home, the situation had changed. The cars that had been bumper-to-bumper kerb-to-kerb were gone. They were within earshot; he could hear the horns blaring off somewhere around Beverly Boulevard and La Cienega, but there was not a car in sight.

Then he came across one. It was lying on its side. He looked down into the windows, dreading what he might see. It was empty. He could not understand how the vehicle had been overturned, because no one could have gone fast enough in the jam to hit anything and be overturned. Besides, he would have heard the crash. Somebody – somebodies – had rocked it back and forth and then pushed it over. Why? He would probably never know.

The signal lights at the intersection were out. He could see well enough across the street to make out the thin dark shape of the pole. Its lights were not operating. When he got to the foot of the light pole on his corner, he saw why. Broken plastic, which would have been green, red and yellow under more lightened circumstances, lay scattered about.

He stood for a while on the kerb and peered into the sickly grey. If a car were to speed down the street without lights, it could be on him before he could get across the street. Nobody but a damned fool would go fast or without lights, but there were many damned fools driving the streets of Los Angeles.

The wailing of a siren became stronger, a flashing red light became visible, and an ambulance whizzed by. He looked up and down the street and dashed across, hoping that the light and noise would have made even the damnedest of fools cautious and that anybody following the ambulance would probably be blowing his horn. He got across with only a slight burning of the lungs. The smog was slowly rusting off their lining. His eyes ran as if they were infected.

The sound of bedlam came to him before the hospital building loomed out of the mists. He was stopped by a white-haired man in the uniform of a security guard. Perhaps the old man had worked at an aircraft plant or at a bank as a guard and had been deputized by the

35

police to serve at the hospital. He flashed his light into Childe's face and asked him if he could help him. The smog was not dark enough to make the light brilliant, but it did annoy Childe.

He said, 'Take that damned light away! I'm here to offer my services in whatever capacity I'm needed.'

He opened his wallet and showed his ID.

The guard said, 'You better go in the front way. The emergency room entrance is jammed, and they're all too busy to talk to you.'

'Who do I see?' Childe said.

The guard hurriedly gave the supervisor's name and directions for getting to his office. Childe entered the lobby and saw at once that his help might be needed, but he was going to have to force it on the hospital. The lobby was jammed and asprawl with people who had been shunted out of the emergency room after more or less complete treatment, relatives of the wounded, people enquiring after lost or injured friends or relatives, and a number who, like Childe, had come to offer their services. The hall outside the supervisor's office was crowded too thickly for him to ram his way through even if he had felt like doing so. He asked a man on the fringes how long he had been trying to get into the office.

'An hour and ten minutes, Mister,' the man said disgustedly.

Childe turned to walk away. He would return to his apartment and do whatever he could to pass the time. Then he would return after a reasonable amount of time (if there were such a thing in this situation), with the hope that some order would have been established. He stopped. There, standing near the front door of the hospital, his head wrapped in a white cloth, was Hamlet Jeremiah.

The cloth could have been a turban, because the last time Childe had seen Jeremiah he was sporting a turban with a spangled hexagram. But the cloth was a bandage with a three-pointed scarlet badge, almost a triskelion. The Mephisthophelean moustaches and beard were gone, and he was wearing a grease-smeared T-shirt with the motto: NOLI ME TANGERE SIN AMOR. His pants were white duck, and brown sandals were on his feet.

'Herald Childe!' he called, smiling, and then his face twisted momentarily as if the smile had hurt.

Childe held out his hand.

Jeremiah said, 'You touch me with love?'

'I'm very fond of you, Ham,' Childe said, 'although I can't really say why. Do we have to go through that at this time?'

'Any time and all time,' Jeremiah said. 'Especially this time.'

'OK. It's love then,' and Childe shook his head. 'What in hell happened? What're you doing down here? Listen, did you know I tried to phone you a little while ago and I was thinking about driving up to see you. Then . . .'

Jeremiah held up his hand and laughed and said, 'One thing at a time! I'm out of my Sunset pad because my wives insisted we get out of town. I told them we ought to wait a day or so until the roads were cleared. By then, the smog'd be gone, anyway, or on its way out. But they wouldn't listen. They cried and carried on something awful, unreeled my entrails and tromped on them. One good thing about tears; they wash out the smog, keep the acids from eating up your corneas. But they're also acid on the nerves, so I said, finally, OK, I love you both, so we'll take off. But if we get screwed up or anything bad happens, don't blame me. Stick it up your own lovely asses. So they smiled and wiped away the tears and packed up and we took off down Doheny. Sheila had a little hand-operated prayer wheel spinning and Lupe was getting three roaches out so we could enjoy what would otherwise be a real drag, or so we at least could enjoy a facsimile of joy. We came to Melrose, and the light changed to red, so I stopped, being a lawabiding citizen when the law is for the benefit of all and well-founded. Besides, I didn't want to get run into. But the son of Adam behind me got mad; he thought I ought to run the light. His soul was really ruffled, Herald, he was in a cold-sweat panic. He honked his horn and when I didn't jump like a dog through a hoop and go through the light, he jumped out of his car and opened my door – dumb bastard, I didn't have it locked – and he jerked me out and whirled me around and shoved my head against the handle. It cut my head open and knocked me half-silly. Naturally, I didn't resist; I really believe this turn-the-other-cheek dictum.

'I was half in the next lane, and the other cars weren't going to stop, so Sheila jumped out and shoved the man in the path of one and pulled me into the car. That Sheila has a temper, you got to forgive her. The man was hit; he bounced off one car and into ours. So Sheila drove the car then while Lupe was trying to heave the man out. He was lying on the back seat with his legs dragging on the street. I stopped her and told Sheila to take us to the hospital.

'So she did, though reluctantly, I mean reluctantly to take the man, too, and we got here, and my head finally got bandaged, and Sheila and Lupe are helping the nurses up on the second floor. I'll help as soon as I get to feeling better.'

'What happened to the man?' Childe said.

'He's on a mattress on the floor of the second level. He's unconscious, breathing a few bubbles of blood, poor unhappy soul, but Sheila's taking care of him, too. She feels bad about shoving him; she's got a hasty temper but underneath it all she truly loves.'

'I was going to offer to help,' Childe said, 'but I can't see standing around for hours. Besides . . .'

Jeremiah asked him what the *besides* meant. Childe told him about Colben and the film. Jeremiah was shocked. He said that he had heard a little about it over the radio. He had not received a paper for two days, so he had no chance to read anything about it. Childe wanted somebody with a big library on vampires and on other things that boomp in the unlit halls of the mind?

Well, he knew just the man. And he lived not more than six blocks away, just south of Wilshire. If anybody would have the research material, it would be Woolston Heepish.

'Isn't he likely to be trying to get out of town?'

'Woolie? By Dracula's moustache, no! Nothing, except maybe an atomic attack threat, would get him to desert his collection. Don't worry; he'll be home. There *is* one problem. He doesn't like unexpected visitors, you got to phone him ahead of time and ask if you can come, even his best friends - except may be for D. Nimming Rodder - are no exceptions. Everybody phones and asks permission, and if he isn't expecting you, he usually won't answer the doorbell. But he knows my voice; I'll holler through the door at him.'

'*Rodder*? Where have . . . ? Oh, yes! The book and TV writer! Vampires, werewolves, a lovely young girl trapped in a hideous old mansion high on a hill, that sort of thing. He produced and wrote the *Shadow Land* series, right?'

'Please, Herald, don't say anything at all about him if you can't say something good. Woolie worships D. Nimming Rodder. He won't hit you if you say anything disparaging about him, but you sure as Shiva won't get any co-operation and you'll find yourself frozen out.'

Childe shifted from one foot to another and coughed. The cough was only partly from the burning air. It indicated that he was having a struggle with his conscience. He wanted to stay here and help - part of him did - but the other part, the more powerful, wanted to get out and away on the trail. Actually, he couldn't be much use here, not for some time, anyway. And he had a feeling, only a feeling but one which had ended in something objectively profitable in the past, that something down there in the dark deeps was nibbling at his hook.

He put his hand on Jeremiah's bony shoulder and said, 'I'll try to phone him, but if . . .'

'No use, Herald. He has an answering service, and it's not likely that'll be working now.'

'Give me a note of introduction, so I can get my foot in the door.'

Jeremiah smiled and said, 'I'll do better than that. I'll walk with you to Woolie's. I'm just in the way here, and I'd like to get away from the sight of so much suffering.'

'I don't know,' Childe said. 'You could have a concussion. Maybe you . . .'

Jeremiah shrugged and said, 'I'm going with you. Just a minute while I find the women and tell them where I'm going.'

Childe, waiting for him, and having nothing to do but watch and listen, understood why Jeremiah wanted to get away. The blood and the groans and weeping were bad enough, but the many chopping coughs and loud, long pumping-up-snot-or-blood coughs irritated, perhaps even angered him, although the anger was rammed far down. He did not know why coughs set him on edge so much, but he knew that Sybil's nicotine cough and burbling lungs, occurring at any time of day or night and especially distressing when he was eating or making love, had caused their split as much as anything. Or had made him believe so.

Jeremiah seemed to skate through the crowd. He took Childe's hand and led him out the front door. It was three minutes after 12.00. The sun was a distorted yellow-greenish lobe. A man about a hundred feet east of them was a wavering shadowy figure. There seemed to be thick and thin bands of smog sliding past each other and thus darkening and lightening, squeezing and elongating objects and people. This must have been an illusion or some other phenomenon, because the smog was not moving. There was not a rumour of a breeze. The heat seemed to filter down through the green-greyishness, to slide down the filaments of smog like acrobats with fevers and sprawl outwards and wrap themselves around people.

Childe's armpits and back and face were wet but the perspiration only cooled him a little. His crotch and his feet were also sweating, and he wished that he could wear swimming trunks or a towel. It was better outside than in the hospital, however. The stench of sweaty frightened people had been powerful, but the noise and the sight of the misery and pain had made it less offensive. Now he was aware that Jeremiah, who was, despite being a 'hippie', a lover of baths, a true 'water brother' as he liked to say, stank. The odour was a peculiar combination of pipe tobacco, marijuana, a pungent heavy unidentifiable something suggestive of spermatic fluid, incense, a soupçon of rosewater on cunt, frightened sweat, extrusion of excited shit, and, perhaps, inhaled smog being sweat out.

Jeremiah looked at Childe, coughed, smiled, and said, 'You smell like something washed up out of the Pacific deeps and two weeks dead yourself, if you'll forgive my saying so.'

Childe, although startled, did not comment. Jeremiah had given too many evidences of telepathy or mind-reading. However, there were other explanations which Childe did not really believe. Childe's expression could have told Jeremiah what he was thinking, although Childe would have said that his face was unreadable.

He walked along with Jeremiah. They seemed to be in a tunnel that grew out of the pavement before them and fell flat on to the pavement behind them. Childe felt unaccountably happy for a moment despite the sinus ache, throat and eye burn, insidious crisping of lungs, and stabbing in his testicles. He had not really wanted to be a good servant in the hospital; he had wanted to be sniffing on the track of criminals.

6

'You see, Ham,' Childe said, 'the vampire motif in the film could mean nothing – as a clue – but I feel that it's very important and, in fact, the only thing I can follow up. But the chances . . .'

His voice died. He and Jeremiah stood on the kerb of the north side of Burton Way and waited. The cars were like elephants in the greyness, grey elephants with trunks to tails, huge eyes glowing in the gloom. The lanes here were one-way for westward traffic, but all traffic was moving eastward.

There was only one thing to do if they wished to cross today. Childe stepped out into the traffic. The cars were going so slowly that it was easy to climb up on the hood of the nearest and jump over on to the next hood and on to a third and then a fourth and on to the grass of the divider.

Startled and outraged drivers and passengers cursed and howled at them, but Jeremiah only laughed and Childe jeered at them. They crossed the divider and jumped from hood to hood again until they got to the other side. They walked down Willaman, and every house was unlit. At Wilshire and Willaman, the street lights were operating, but the cars were paying no attention. All were going eastward on both sides of Wilshire.

The traffic was a little faster here but not too fast. Childe and Jeremiah got over, although Jeremiah slipped once and fell on top of a hood.

'Middle of this block,' Jeremiah said.

The houses and apartments were middle middle-class. The homes were the usual California–Spanish bungalows; the apartment buildings were four or five storey boxes with some attempts at decoration and terracing outside. There were lights in a few windows but the house before which Jeremiah stopped was dark.

'Must not be home,' Childe said.

'Doesn't mean a thing. His windows are always dark. Once you get inside, you'll see why. He may not be home just now; he might've gone to the store or the gas station; they're supposed to be open, at least the governor said they would. Let's see.'

They crossed the yard. The front window looked boarded up. At least, something dark and woody looking covered it on the inside.

41

Closer, he saw that the man-sized figure, which had stood so silently and which he had thought was an iron statue, was a wooden and painted cutout of Godzilla.

They went around the side of the house to the driveway. There was a large red sign with glaring yellow letters: MISTER HORROR IS ALIVE AND WELL IN HERE.

Beyond was a sort of courtyard with a tree which bent at forty-five degrees and the top of which covered the porch roof and part of the house roof like a great greenish hand. The tree trunk was so grey and twisted and knobbed that Childe thought for a moment that it was artificial. It looked as if it had been designed and built as background to a horror movie.

There were many signs on the door and the walls beside the door, some of them 'cute' and others 'in' jokes. There were also masks of Frankenstein's Monster, Dracula, and the Wolf-Man nailed against the walls. And several NO SMOKING ABSOLUTELY signs. Another forbade any alcoholic beverages to be brought in.

Jeremiah pressed the button, which was the nose of a gargoyle face painted around it. A loud clanging noise as of large bells came from within and then several bars of organ music: *Gloomy Sunday.*

There was no other response. Jeremiah waited a moment and then rang the bell again. More bells and organ music. But no one at the door.

Jeremiah beat on the door and shouted, 'Open up, Woolie! I know you're in there! It's OK! It's me, Hamlet Jeremiah, one of your greatest fans!'

The little peep-window slid back and light rayed out. The light was cut off, came back, was cut off again as the peep-window swung shut. The door opened with a screeching of rusty hinges. A few seconds later, Childe understood that the noise was a recording.

'Welcome,' a soft baritone said. Jeremiah tapped Childe's shoulder to indicate he should precede him. They walked in, and the man shut the door, rammed home three large bolts, and hooked two chains.

The room was too confusing for Childe to take it in all at once. He concentrated on the man, whom Jeremiah introduced as Woolston Q. Heepish.

'Woolie' was about six feet in height, portly and soft-looking, moderately paunched, with a bag of skin hanging under his chin, bronze walrus moustache, square rimless spectacles, a handsome profile from the mouth up, a full head of dark-red, straight, slick hair, and pale grey eyes. He hunched forward as if he had spent most of his life over a desk.

The walls and windows of the room were covered with shelves of books and various objects and with paintings, movie stills, posters, masks, plastic busts, framed letters, and blow-ups of movie actors. There was a sofa, several chairs, and a grand piano. The room beyond looked much the same except for its lack of furniture.

If he wanted to learn about vampires, he was at the right place.

The place was jammed with anything and everything concerning Gothic literature, folklore, legendry, the supernatural, lycanthropy, demonology, witch-craft, and the movies made of these subjects.

Woolie shook Childe's hand with a large, wet, plump hand.

'Welcome to the House of Horror,' he said.

Jeremiah explained why they were there. Woolie shook his head and said that he had heard about Colben over the radio. The announcer had said that Colben had been 'horribly mutilated' but he had not given any details.

Childe told him the details. Heepish shook his head and tsk-tsked while his grey eyes seemed to get brighter and the corners of his lips dimpled.

'How terrible! How awful! Sickening! My God, the savages still in our midst! How can such things be?'

The soft voice murmured and seemed to become lost, as if it were breaking up into a half dozen parts which, like mice, scurried for the dark in the corners. The pale, soft wet hands rubbed together now and then and several times were clasped in a gesture which at first looked prayerful but also gave the impression of being placed around an invisible neck.

'If there is anything I can do to help you track down these monsters; if there is anything in my house to help you, you are welcome,' Heepish said. 'Though I can't imagine what kind of clue you could find by just browsing through. Still . . .'

He spread both hands out and then said, 'But let me conduct you through my house. I always have the guided tour first for strangers. Hamlet can come with us or look around on his own, if he wishes. Now, this blow-up here is of Alfred Dummel and Else Bennrich in the German film, *The Blood Drinker*, made in 1928. It had a rather limited distribution in this country, but I was fortunate enough – I have many many friends all over the world and even in Germany – to get a print of the film. It may be the only print now existing; I've made enquiries and never been able to locate another, and I've had many people trying to find another for me . . .'

Childe restrained the impulse to tell Heepish that he wanted to see the newspaper files at once. He did not wish to waste any time. But Jeremiah had told him how he must behave if he wanted to get maximum co-operation from his host.

The house was crammed with objects of many varieties, all originating in the world of terror and evil shadows but designed and manufactured to make money. The house was bright with illuminations of many shades: bile-yellow, blood-red, decay-purple, rigor mortis-greyblue, repressed-anger orange, but shadows seemed to press in everywhere. Where no shadow could be, there was shadow.

An air-conditioner was moving air slowly and icily, as if the next glacial age were announcing itself. The air was well-filtered, because the burning of eyes and throat and lungs was fading. (Something good to say about ice ages.) Despite this, and the ridges of skin pinched by cold air, Childe felt as if he were suffocating with the closeness and bulk and disorder of the books, the masks, the heads of movie monsters, the distorted wavy menacing paintings, the Frankenstein monsters and Wolf-Men dolls, the little Revolting Robot toys, the Egyptian statues of jackal-headed Anubis, the cat-headed Sekhmet.

The room beyond was smaller but also much more cluttered.

Woolie gestured vaguely – at the leaning and sometimes collapsed piles of books and magazines.

'I got a shipment in from a collector in Utica. New York,' Heepish said. 'He died recently.'

His voice deepened and richened almost to oiliness. 'Very sad. A fine man. A real fan of the horror. We corresponded for years, more than I care to say, although I never actually got to meet him. But our minds met, we had much in common. His widow sent me this stuff, told me to price it at whatever I thought was fair. There's a complete collection of *Weird Tales* from 1923 through 1954, a first edition of Chambers's *King in Yellow*, a first edition of *Dracula* with a signature from Bram Stoker and Bela Lugosi, and, oh! there is so so much!'

He rubbed his hands and smiled. 'So much! But the prize is a letter from Doctor Polidori – he was Byron's personal physician and friend, you know – author of an anonymous book – I have several first editions of the first vampire novel in English – *The Vampyre*. Doctor Polidori! A letter from him to a Lady Milbanks describing how he got

44

the idea for his novel! It's unique! I've been lusting – literally lusting – for it ever since I heard about it in 1941! It'll occupy a prominent place – perhaps the most prominent – on the front room wall as soon as I can get a suitable frame!'

Childe refrained from asking where he would find a bare place on the wall.

Heepish showed him his office, a large room with living dimensions constricted by many rows of ceiling-high bookcases and by a huge old-fashioned rolltop desk engulfed by books, magazines, letters, maps, stills, posters, statuettes, toys, and a headsman's axe that looked genuine, even to the dried blood.

They went back to the room between the office and living room, where Heepish led Childe into the kitchen. This had a stove, a sink, and a refrigerator, but otherwise was full of books, magazines, small filing cases, and some dead insects on the edges of the open cupboards and on the floor.

'I'm having the stove taken out next week,' Heepish said. 'I don't eat in, and when I give a party, I have everything brought in.'

Childe raised his eyebrows but said nothing. Jeremiah had told him that the refrigerator was so full of microfilms that there was little room for food. And at the rate the film was coming in, there would soon not be space enough for a quart of milk.

'I am thinking about building an extension to my house,' Heepish said. 'As you can see, I'm a teeny-weeny bit crowded now, and heaven knows what it will be like five years from now. Or even one.'

Woolston Heepish had been married – for over fifteen years. His wife had wanted children, but he had said no. Children could not be kept away from his books, magazines, paintings and drawings, masks and costumes, toys and statuettes. Little children were very destructive.

After some years, his wife gave up her wish to have babies. Could she have a pet, a cat or a dog? Heepish said that he was indeed very sorry, but cats clawed and dogs chewed and piddled.

The collection increased; the house shrank. Furniture was removed to make room for more objects. The day came when there was no room for Mrs Heepish. *The Bride of Frankenstein* was elbowing her out. She knew better than to appeal for even a halt to the collecting, and a diminution was unthinkable. She moved out and got a divorce, naming as co-respondent *The Creature From The Black Lagoon*.

It was only fair to Heepish, Jeremiah had said, to let Childe know

45

that Heepish and his wife were the best of friends and went out together as much as when they had lived together. Perhaps, though, this was the ex-Mrs Heepish's way of getting revenge, because she certainly rode herd on him, and he meekly submitted with only a few grumbles now and then.

Now Heepish himself was being forced out. One day, he would come home after a late meeting of *The Count of Dracula Society* and open the front door, and tons of books, magazines, documents, photographs, and bric-a-brac would cascade out, and the rescuers would tunnel down to find Woolston Heepish pressed flat between the leaves of *The Castle of Otranto.*

Childe was led into an enclosed back porch, jammed with books like the other rooms. They stepped out the back door into a pale green light and an instant sensation as of diluted sulphuric acid fumes scraping the eyes. Childe blinked, and his eyes began to run. He coughed. Heepish coughed.

Heepish said, 'Perhaps we should pass up the grand tour of the garage, but . . .'

His voice trailed off. Childe had stopped for a moment; Heepish was a figure as dark and bulky and shapeless as a monster in the watery mists of a grade-B movie.

The door squeaked upward. Childe hastened to enter the garage. The door squeaked down and clanged shut. Childe wondered if this door, too, were connected to a recording taken from the old *Inner Sanctum* radio programme. Heepish turned on the lights. More of the same except that there was dust on the heads, masks, books, and magazines.

'I keep my duplicates, second-rate things, and stuff I just don't have room for in the house at the moment,' Heepish said. Childe felt that he was expected to ejaculate over at least a few items. He wanted to get out of the hot, close and dead air into the house. He hoped that the files he wanted were not stored here.

Childe commented on an entire bookshelf dedicated to the works of D. Nimming Rodder.

Heepish said, 'Oh, you noticed that he is the only living author with an individual placard in my collection in the house? Nim is my favourite, of course, I think he's the greatest writer of all time, in the Gothic or horror genre, even greater than Monk Lewis or H. P. Lovecraft or Bram Stoker. He is a very good friend of mine.

'I keep many duplicates of his works out here because he needs one now and then to use as tearsheets or reference for a new anthology. He has had many anthologies, you know, just scads of reprints and collections taken from his collections, and collections from these. He's probably the most recollected man on Earth.'

Childe did not smile. Heepish shrugged.

There was a large blow-up of Rodder tacked to an upright. In heavy black ink below: TO MY FIRST FAN AND A GREAT FRIEND, MISTER HORROR HIMSELF, WITH INTENSE AFFECTION FROM NIM. The thin, pale face with the collapsed cheeks, sharp nose, and the huge-rimmed spectacles looked like that of a spooky and spooked primate of the Madagascar jungle, like a lemur's. And lemur, now that Childe considered it, originally meant a ghost. He grinned. He remembered the entry in the big unabridged dictionary he had referred to so often at college.

Lemur – Latin *lemures* nocturnal spirits, ghosts; akin to Greek *lamia*, a devouring monster, *lamas* crop, maw, *lamia*, pl., chasm, Lettish *lamata* mousetrap; basic idea: open jaws.

7

Childe, looking at Rodder's photograph, grinned widely.

Heepish said, 'What's so funny? I could stand a little laugh in these trying times.'

'Nothing, really.'

'Don't you like Rodder?'

Heepish's voice was controlled, but it contained a hint of a well-oiled mousetrap aching to snap shut.

Childe said, 'I liked his *Shadow Land* series. And I liked his underlying themes, aside from the spooky element. You know, the *little* man fighting bravely against conformity, authoritarianism, vast forces of corruption, and so on, the lone individual, the only honest man in the world – I liked those things. And every time I read an article in the newspapers about Rodder, he's always described as honest, as a man of integrity. Which is really ironic.'

Childe stopped and then, not wishing to continue but impelled to, said, 'But I know a guy . . .'

He stopped. Why tell Heepish that the *guy* was Jeremiah?

'This guy was at a party which consisted mainly of science-fiction people. He was standing within earshot of a group of authors. One was the great fantasy writer, Breyleigh Bredburger. You know of him, of course?'

Heepish nodded and said, 'After Rodder, Monk Lewis, and Bloch, my favourite.'

Childe said, 'Another author, I forget his name, was complaining that Rodder had stolen one of his magazine stories for his series. Just lifted it, changed the title and a few things, credited it to somebody with an outlandish Greek name, and had, so far, refused to correspond with the author about the alleged theft. Bredburger said that was nothing. Rodder had stolen three of his stories, giving credit to himself, Rodder, as author. Bredburger cornered Rodder twice and forced him to admit the theft and to pay him. Rodder's excuse was that he'd signed to write two-thirds of the series himself and he wasn't up to it, so, in desperation, he'd lifted Bredburger's stories. He didn't say anything about plagiarizing from other people of course. Bredburger said he'd been promised payment for the third stolen story but so far hadn't got it and wouldn't unless he vigorously pursued Rodder or went through the courts.

'A third author then said that the first would have to stand in line behind about twenty if he wanted to sue or to take it out of Rodder's hide.

'That's your D. Nimming Rodder. Your great champion of the *little* man, of the nonconformist, of the *honest* man.'

Childe stopped. He was surprised that he had run on so. He did not want to quarrel. After all, he was to be indebted to this man, if this grand tour ever ended. On the other hand, he was itchy with anger. He had seen too many corrupt men highly honoured by the world, which either did not know the truth or ignored it. Also, the irritation caused by the smog, the repressed panic arising from fear of what the smog might become, Colben's death, the frustrating scene with Sybil, and Heepish's attitude, undefinedly prickly, combined to wear away the skin and fat over his nerves.

Heepish's grey eyes seemed to retreat, as if they were afraid they might combust if they got too close to the light and air. His neck quivered. His moustache drew down; invisible weights had been tied to each end. His nostrils flared like bellows. His pale skin had become red. His hands clenched.

Childe waited while the silence hardened like bird lime. If Heepish got nasty, he would get just as nasty, even though he would lose access to the literature he needed. Childe had been told by Jeremiah that Heepish had got the idea for his collection from observing a man by the name of Forrest J. Ackerman, who had probably the greatest private collection of science-fiction and fantasy in the world. In fact, Heepish had been called the poor man's Ackerman, though not to his face. However, he was far from poor, he had much money – from what source nobody knew – and his collection would someday be the world's greatest, private or public.

But at this moment he was very vulnerable, and Childe was willing to thrust through the crack in the armour.

'Well!' Heepish said.

He cocked his head and smiled thinly. The moustache, however, was still swelled like an elephant seal in mating season, and his fingers were making a steeple, then separating to form the throat-holding attitude.

'Well!' he said again. His voice was as hard, but there was also a whine in it, like a distant mosquito.

'Well!' Childe said, aware that he would never know what Heepish

49

was going to say and not caring. 'I'd like to see the newspaper files, if possible.'

'Oh? Oh, yes! They're upstairs. This way, please.'

They left the garage, but Heepish put the photograph of Rodder under his arm before following him out. Childe had wondered what it was doing out in the garage, anyway, but on re-entering the house, he saw that there were many more photographs – and paintings and pencil sketches and even framed newspaper and magazine clippings containing Rodder's portrait – than he had thought. Heepish had had one too many and stored that one in the garage. But now, as if to show Childe his place, to put him down in some obscure manner, Heepish was also bringing this photograph into the house.

Childe grinned at this as he waited for Heepish to lead him through the kitchen and hall-room and turn right to go up the narrow stairs. The walls were hung with many pictures and paintings of Frankenstein's monster and Dracula and an original by Hannes Bok and another by Virgil Finlay, all leaning at slightly different angles like headstones in an old neglected graveyard.

They went down a short hallway and into a room with the walls covered with paintings and photographs and posters and movie ad stills. There were a number of curious wooden frames, sawhorses with castles on their backs, which held a series of illustrations and photos and newspaper clippings on wooden frames. These could be turned on a central shaft, like pages of a book.

Childe looked through all of them and, at any other time, would have been delighted and would have lingered over various nostalgic items.

Heepish, as if the demands on him were really getting to be too much, sighed when Childe asked to see the scrapbooks. He went into an enormous closet the walls of which were lined with bookshelves stuffed with large scrapbooks, many of them dusty and smelling of decay.

'I really must do something about these before it's too late,' Heepish said. 'I have some very valuable – some invaluable and irreplaceable – material here.'

He was still carrying Rodder's photo under one arm.

It was Childe's turn to sigh as he looked at the growing hill of stuff to peruse. But he sat down in a chair, placed his right ankle over his left thigh, and began to turn the stiff and often yellowed and brittle pages of the scrapbooks. After a while, Heepish said that he would have to excuse himself. If Childe wanted anything, he should just holler. Childe looked up and smiled briefly and said that he did not want to be any more bother than he had to be. Heepish was gone then, but left an almost visible ectoplasm of disdain and hurt feelings behind him.

The scrapbooks were titled with various subjects: MOVIE VAMPIRES, GERMAN AND SCANDINAVIAN, 1919-1939; WEREWOLVES, AMERICAN, 1865-1900; WITCHES, PENN-SYLVANIAN, 1880-1965; GOLEM, EXTRAFORTEANA,1929-1960; SOUTHERN CALIFORNIA VAMPIRE FOLKLORE AND GHOST STORIES, 1910-1967; and so on.

Childe had gone through thirty-two such titles before he came to the last one. They had all been interesting but not very fruitful, and he did not *know* that the one which was in his hands was relevant. But he felt his heart quicken and his back become less stiff. It could not be called a clue, but it at least was something to investigate.

An article from the *Los Angeles Times*, dated 1 May, 1958, described a number of reputedly 'haunted' houses in the Los Angeles area. Several long paragraphs were devoted to a house in Beverly Hills which not only had a ghost, it had a 'vampire'.

There was a photograph of the Trolling House taken from the air. According to the article, no one could get close enough to it on the ground to use a camera effectively. The house was set on a low hill in the middle of a large – for Southern California – walled estate. The grounds were well wooded so that the house could not be seen from anywhere outside the walls. The newspaper cameramen had been unable to get photos of it in 1948, when the owner of Trolling House had become temporarily famous, and the newsmen had no better luck in 1958, when this article, recapitulating the events of ten years before, had been published. There was, however, a picture of a pencil sketch made of the 'vampire', Baron Igescu, by an artist who had depended upon his memory after seeing the baron at a charity ball. Very few people had seen the baron, although he had made several appearances at charity balls and once at a Beverly Hills taxpayers' protest meeting.

Trolling House was named after the uncle of the present owner. The uncle, also an Igescu, had travelled from Rumania to England in 1887, stayed there one year, and then moved on to America in 1889. Upon becoming a citizen of the United States of America, Igescu had changed his name to Trolling. No one knew why. The mansion was on woodland surrounded on all sides by a high brick wall topped with iron spikes between which barbed wire was strung. Built in very late Victorian style in 1900 in what was then out-of-the-way agricultural land, it was a huge rambling structure. The nucleus was a part of the original house. This was, naturally, a Spanish-style mansion which had been built by the eccentric (some said, mad) Don Pedro del Osorojo in the wilderness of what was to become, a century later, Beverly Hills. Del Osorojo was supposed to have been a relative of the de Villa family, which owned this area, but that was not authenticated. Actually little was known of del Osorojo except that he was a recluse with an unknown source of wealth. His wife came from Spain (this was at a time that California was under Spanish rule) and was supposed to have been of Castilian nobility.

The present owner, Igescu, was involuntarily publicized in 1938 when he was brought dead-on-arrival into the Cedars of Lebanon Hospital after a car collision at Hollywood and La Brea. At twilight of the following day, the country coroner was to perform an inquest. Igescu had no perceptible wounds or injuries.

At the first touch of the knife, Igescu sat up on the dissection slab.

This story was picked up by newspapers throughout the States because a reporter jestingly pointed out that Igescu had (1) never been seen in the daytime, (2) was of Carpathian origin, (3) came from an aristocratic family which had lived for centuries in a castle (now abandoned) on top of a high steep hill in a remote rural area, (4) had shipped his uncle's body back to the old country to be buried in the family tomb, but the coffin had disappeared en route, and (5) was living in a house already well-known because of the ghost of Dolores del Osorojo.

Dolores was supposedly the spirit of Don Pedro's daughter. She had died of grief, or killed herself because of grief. Her lover, or suitor, was a Norwegian sea-captain who had seen Dolores at a governor's ball during one of her rare appearances in town. He seemed to have lost his sanity over her. He neglected his ship and its business, and his men deserted or were thrown into the local jail for drunkenness and vagrancy.

Lars Ulf Larsson, the captain, barred by the old don from seeing Dolores, managed to sneak into the house and woo her so successfully that she promised to run off with him within a week. But the night of the elopement came, and Larsson did not show up. He was never seen again; a legend had it that Don Pedro had killed him and buried his body on the estate. Another said that the body had been thrown into the sea.

Dolores had gone into mourning and died several weeks later. Her father went hunting into the hills several weeks after she was buried and failed to return. Search parties could not find him; it was said that the Devil had taken him.

Later occupants of the house reported that they sometimes saw Dolores in the house or out on the lawn. She was always dressed in a black formal gown of the 1800s and had black hair, a pale skin, and very red lips. Her appearances were not frequent, but they were nerve-racking enough to cause a long line of tenants and owners to move out. The old mansion had fallen into ruins, except for two rooms, when Uncle Igescu bought the property and built his house around the still-standing part.

Despite the publicity about the present Igescu, not much was really known about him. He had inherited a chain of grocery stores and an export business from his uncle. He, or his managers, had built the stores into a large chain of supermarkets in the Southwest and had expanded the export business.

Childe found the ghost interesting. Whether or not she had been seen recently was not known, because neither Igescu had ever said anything about her. Her last recorded appearance was in 1878, when the Reddes had moved out.

Igescu's sketch in the newspaper showed a long lean face with a high forehead and high cheekbones and large eyes and thick eyebrows. He had a thick downdrooping Slovak coalminer's type of moustache.

Heepish returned, and Childe, holding the sketch so he could see it, said, 'This man certainly doesn't look Draculaish does he? More like the grocery store man, which he is, right?'

Heepish poked his head forward and squinted his eyes. He smiled slightly. 'Certainly, he doesn't look like Bela Lugosi. But the Dracula of the book, Bram Stoker's, had just such a moustache. Or one like it, anyway. I tried to get in touch with Igescu several times, you know, but I couldn't get through his secretary. She was nice but very firm. The Baron did not want to be disturbed with any such nonsense.'

Heepish's tone and weak hollow chuckle said that, if there were any nonsense, it was on the Baron's part.

'You have his phone number?'

'Yes, but it took me a lot of trouble to get it. It's unlisted.'

'You don't owe him anything,' Childe said, 'I'd like to have it. If I find anything you might be interested in, I'll tell you. How's that? I feel I owe you something for your time and fine co-operation. Perhaps, I might be able to dig up something for your collection.'

'Well, you can have the number,' Heepish said, warming up. 'But it's probably been changed.'

He conducted Childe downstairs and, while Childe waited under a shelf which held the heads of Frankenstein's monster, The Naked Brain, and a huge nameless creature from some (deservedly) forgotten movie, Heepish plunged into the rear of the house down a dim corridor with plastic cobwebs between ceiling and wall. He dived out of the shadows and webs with a little black book in his hand. Childe wrote down the number and address in his own little black book and asked permission to try the number. He dialled and got what he expected, a busy signal. The lines were still tied up, unless, that is, he had got through to Igescu's and Igescu's phone was busy. He tried the LAPD number. That was busy. He tried his own phone, and there was a clicking, and then only a hum.

Just for stubbornness, he tried Igescu's number again. And this time, as if the fates had decided that he should be favoured, or by one of those coincidences too implausible to be believed in a novel but sometimes happening in 'real' life, the connection went through. A woman's voice said, 'Hello? My God, the lines aren't busy anymore! What happened?'

'May I speak to Baron Igescu?' Childe said.

'Who?'

'Isn't this Baron Igescu's residence?'

'No! Who is this speaking?'

'Herald Wellston,' Childe said, giving the name he had decided to use. 'May I ask who is speaking?'

'Go away! Or I'll call the police!' the woman screamed, and she hung up.

'I don't think that was Igescu's secretary,' Childe said in answer to Heepish's quizzical expression. 'Somebody else has their number now.'

Not believing that it would work but willing to try, he dialled information. The call went right through, and he succeeded almost immediately in getting transferred to his contact. She did not have to worry about a supervisor listening in; she was the supervisor.

'What happened, Linda? All of a sudden the lines're wide open.'

'I don't know, one of the unexplainable lulls, the eye of the storm, maybe. But it won't last, you can bet your most precious possession on that, Herald. You better hurry.'

He told her what he wanted, and she got Igescu's unlisted number for him within a few seconds.

'I'll drop off the usual to you in the mail before evening. Thanks, Linda, you beautiful beautiful.'

'I may not be here to get it if this smog keeps up,' she said. 'Or the mailman may have skipped town with everyone and his brother.'

He hung up the telephone. Heepish, who had stepped out of the room but not out of hearing range, raised his eyebrows. Childe did not feel that he had to justify himself, but, since he was using Heepish's phone, he did owe him some explanation.

'The forces of good must use corruption to fight corruption,' he said. 'I occasionally have to find a number, and I send a ten to my informant, or used to; now it's a twenty, what with inflation. In this case, I suspect I've wasted my money.'

Heepish harrumphed. Childe got out quickly; he felt as if he could no longer stand this shadowy, musky place with its monsters frozen in various attitudes of attack and their horrified paralysed victims. Nor could he endure the custodian of the museum any longer.

Yet, when he stood at the door to say good-bye and to thank his host, he felt ashamed. Certainly, the man's hobby – passion, rather – was harmless enough and even entertaining – even emotionally purgative – for millions of children and adults who had never quite ceased being children. Though dedicated to archetypal horror and its Hollywood sophisticated developments, the house had defeated itself, hence, had a therapeutic value. Where there is a surfeit of horrors, horror becomes hokum.

And this man had helped him to the best of his ability.

He thanked Heepish and shook his hand, and perhaps Heepish felt the change in his guest, because he smiled broadly and radiated warmth and asked Childe to come back – any time.

The door swung shut with the Inner-Sanctum creakings, but it did not propel Childe and Jeremiah into the acid-droplet mist. A breeze ruffled them, and sunshine was bright, and the sky was blue.

Childe had not known until then how depressed and miserable he had been. Now, he blinked his eyes that did not burn or weep and sucked in the precious clean air. He chortled and did a little jig arm in arm with Jeremiah. The walk back to his apartment was the most delightful walk in his life. Its delight exceeded even that of his first

55

walk with Sybil when he was courting her. The yards and sidewalks held a surprising number of people, all enjoying the air and the sun. Apparently, fewer than he – and the radio and TV experts – had thought had fled the area.

There were, however, few cars on the streets. Wilshire Boulevard held only one auto between La Cienega and Robertson, and when they crossed Burton Way on Willaman, they could see no cars.

However, there were great green-grey clouds piled against the mountains. Pasadena and Glendale and other inland cities were still in the fist of the smog.

By the time he had said good-bye to Jeremiah, who turned off towards Mt Sinai Hospital, the wind had slid to a halt, and the air was as still as a dead jellyfish again. There was a peculiar glow on the western horizon; a hush descended as if a finger had been placed against the lips of the world.

He still felt happy as he went into the apartment building. The phone lines were busy again, but he stuck it out, and, within three hundred seconds by his wristwatch, the phone rang. The voice that answered was female, low, and lovely.

Magda Holyani was Mr Igescu's secretary; she stressed the 'Mister'.

No, Mr Igescu could not talk to him. Mr Igescu never talked to anybody without an appointment. No, he would not grant an interview to Mr Herald Wellston, no matter how far Mr Wellston had travelled for it nor how important the magazine Mr Wellston represented. Mr Igescu never gave interviews, and if Mr Wellston was thinking of that silly vampire and ghost story in the *Times*, he had better forget it – as far as talking to Mr Igescu about it. Or about anything.

And how had Mr Wellston got this unlisted number?

Childe did not answer the last. He asked that his request be forwarded to her employer. She said that he would be informed of it as soon as possible. Childe gave her his number – he said he was staying with a friend – and told her that if Igescu should change his mind, he should call him at that number. He thanked her and hung up. Throughout the conversation, neither had said a word about the smog.

Childe decided to do some thinking, and, while he was doing that, he had better attend to some immediate matters – such as his survival. He drove to the supermarket and found that it had just been reopened. Apparently, the manager was staying on the premises, and several of the checkout women and the liquor store clerk lived nearby. Cars were beginning to fill the parking lot, and people on foot were numerous. Childe was glad that he had thought of this, because the shelves were beginning to look bare. He stocked up on canned goods and powdered milk and purchased a five-gallon bottle of distilled water.

On the way back, he heard six sirens and saw two ambulances. The hospital was not about to complain of lack of business.

By the time he had put away the groceries, he had made up his mind. He would drive out and scout around the Igescu estate. He had no rational cause to do so. There was not the thinnest of threads to connect Igescu with Colben. Nevertheless, he meant to investigate. He had nowhere else to go and nothing to do. He could spend the rest of the day with this doubtless unrewarding lead, and tomorrow, if the city began to return to normal, he would start on a definite and profitable case, if one showed up. And one should. There were bound to be many missing persons, gone somewhere with the smog.

8

The drive out was pleasant. He saw only ten cars on the streets; two were police. The black-and-whites, red lights flashing but sirens quiet, raced past him.

Childe went west on Santa Monica Boulevard, turned right at Rexford Drive, and began the safari through the ever wealthier and more exclusive houses and mansions (northward was the hierarchical goal). He went up Coldwater Canyon and into the hills, which are labelled on the map as the Santa Monica Mountains. He swung left on to Mariconado Lane, drove for a mile and a half on the narrow, winding, macadam road, almost solidly walled with great oaks, firs, and high thick bushes and hedges, turned right on Daimon drive, drove for a mile past several high-walled estates, and came finally to Igescu's (if Heepish had given him correct directions).

At the end of the high brick mortared-with-white wall, three hundred yards past the gateway, the road ended. There were no walls to keep anybody from walking past the end of the drive. Whoever owned the land next to the Baron's felt no need for enforcing privacy. Childe drove to the end of the pavement, and after some manoeuvring, turned the car around. He left it with its rear against a bush and facing the road. If he had to leave suddenly, he would not be delayed by having to go back and forwards several times. After locking the doors, he put an extra key in the earth under a bush (always prepare for emergencies) and then walked to the gateway.

The wall was ten feet high and topped by iron spikes between which were from four to six strands of barbed wire. The gateway was a single heavy iron grille-work which swung out when electrically actuated. He could see no keyholes. A tongue of metal must insert into a slot in a metal fitting in the side of the gateway. The grille-work was painted a dull black and separated into eight squares by thick iron bars. Each square held a sheet of iron formed into the profile of a griffin with the wings of a bat. This was a grade-B movie touch, but, of course, only coincidence. The bat wings probably had some heraldic significance.

A metal box six feet up on the right post could be a voice transceiver. Beyond the gate was a narrow tar-topped road which curved and disappeared into the thick woods. The only sign of life was a listless black squirrel. (The radio had reported that all wild land birds had fled the area.)

Childe walked into the woods at the end of the road. He ignored the TRESPASSERS WILL BE VIGOROUSLY PROSECUTED sign – he liked the VIGOROUSLY – to walk along the wall. The going was not easy. The bushes and thorns seemed determined to hold him back. He shoved against them and wriggled a few times and then the wall curved to the right and went up a steep hill. Panting, he scrambled up on all fours to the top. He wondered if he were that much out of shape or if the smog had cut down his ability to take in enough oxygen.

The wall still barred his way. After resting, he climbed a big oak. Near the top, he looked around, but he could see only more trees beyond the wall. No branches offered passage over the walls.

He climbed down slowly and carefully. When he was a child, he had at times thought that he might prefer to be Lord Greystoke instead of Sherlock Holmes. He had grown up to be neither, but he was much closer to Holmes than Greystoke. He wouldn't even make a good Jane. Sweat ran down his face and soaked his undershirt below the armpits. His pants were torn in two places, a small scratch on the back of his left hand was bleeding, his hands were sore on the palms and dirty all over, and his shoes were badly scuffed. The sun, in sympathetic altitude with his spirits, was low. It was just about to touch the ridge of the western hills he could see through a break. He would have to go back now and conduct a tour of the wall some other time – if ever. To ram and bumble through the woods in the dark would be more than exasperating.

He hastened back to the car, tearing a button off his shirt this time, and got to it just at dusk. The silence was like that in a deep cave. No birds twittered or chirped. Even the buzz and hum of insects were absent. Perhaps the smog had killed them off. Or, at least, thinned their ranks or discouraged them. There were no sounds of aeroplanes or cars, sounds which it had been difficult to escape anywhere in Los Angeles County night or day. The atmosphere seemed heavy with a spirit of – what? – of waiting. Whether it was waiting for him or something else, and what it was waiting for, was dubious. And, after he considered the feeling, he found it ridiculous.

He got into the car behind the wheel, remembered that he had left a key in the dirt under a bush, started to get out to retrieve it, then thought better of it, and closed the door again. He drummed his fingers, wished he had not quit smoking, and chewed some gum. He almost turned the radio on but decided that, in this stillness, its sound would go too far.

The suncast fell away from the sky at last. The darkness around him became thicker, as if it were the sediment of night. The glow thrown by the million lights of the city and reflected back on to the earth was missing tonight. There were no clouds to act as mirrors, and the surrounding hills and trees barred the horizon-shine. Stars began to thrust through the black. After a while, the almost full moon, edged in black, like a card announcing a death, rose above the trees.

Childe waited. He got out after a while and went to the gate and looked through, but he could not even see a faint nimbus which might have revealed that, somewhere in that dense blackness, was a large house with many lights and at least two people. He returned to the car, sat for perhaps fifteen minutes longer, and then reached for the ignition key. His hand stopped an inch from the key.

He heard a sound which turned his scalp cold.

He had hunted enough in Montana and the Yukon to recognize the sound. It was the howling of wolves. It rose from somewhere in the trees behind the walls of Igescu's estate.

9

He was tired when he returned to his apartment. It was only ten P.M. but he had been through much. Besides, the poisoned air had burned away his vitality. The respite of the breeze had not helped much. The air was still dead, and it seemed to him that it was getting grey again. That must be one of the tricks his imagination was playing him, because there were not enough cars on the streets to account for another build-up of smog.

He called the LAPD and asked for Sergeant Bruin. He did not expect Bruin to be there, but he was lucky. Bruin had much to say about his troubles with traffic that day. Not to mention that his wife had suddenly decided to get out of town. For Christ's sake! The smog was gone! For a while, anyway. No telling what would happen if this crazy weather continued. He had to get to bed now, because tomorrow looked even worse. Not the traffic. Most of the refugees should be past the state line by now. But they'd be back. That wasn't what was worrying him. The crazy weather and the smog, the sudden departure of the smog, rather, had resulted in a soaring upward of murders and suicides. He'd talk to Childe tomorrow, if he had time.

'You sound as if you're out on your feet, Bruin,' Childe said. 'Don't you want to hear about what I've been doing on the Colben case?'

'You found out anything definite?' Bruin said.

'I'm on to something, I got a hunch . . .'

'A hunch! A hunch! For God's sake, Childe, I'm tired! See you!' The phone clicked.

Childe cursed, but after a while he had to admit that Bruin's reaction was justified. He decided to go to bed. He checked his automatic-answer device. There was one call. At 9.45, just before he had got home. Magda Holyani had phoned to inform him that Mr Igescu had changed his mind and would grant him an interview. He could call back if he got in before ten. If he didn't, he was not to phone until after three the following afternoon.

Childe could not go to sleep for a long time because of wondering what could have made the Baron change his mind. Could he have seen Childe outside the walls and decided to invite him within for some sinister reason?

He awoke suddenly, sitting up, his heart racing. The phone was ringing on the stand beside him. He knocked it over and had to climb down out of bed to get it off the floor. Sergeant Bruin's voice answered him.

The crooked hands of the clock on the stand touched the Gothic style 12 and 8.

'Childe? Childe. OK! I'd feel bad about getting you up, but I been up since six myself. Listen, Budler's car was found this morning! In the same lot Colben's car was found in, how you like that? The lab boys, what're available, are going over it now.'

'What time in the morning?' Childe said.

'About six, why, what difference does that make? You got something?'

'No. Listen, if you got time,' and Childe outlined what he had done. 'I just wanted you to know that I was going there tonight in case I didn't . . .'

He stopped. He suddenly felt foolish, and Bruin's chuckle deepened the feeling.

'In case you don't report back? Haw! Haw!'

Bruin's laughter was loud. Finally, he said, 'OK, Childe. I'll watch out you check in. But this deal about this vampire – a baron, no shit? A real live Transylvanian vampire-type Rumanian baron, what runs a line of supermarkets, right? Haw! Haw! Childe, you sure the smog ain't been eating away your brain cells?'

'Have your fun,' Childe said dignifiedly. 'Have you got any leads, by the way?'

'How the hell could we? You know we've had no time!'

'What about the wolves, then?' Childe said. 'Isn't there some sort of law about having wild animals, dangerous animals, on the premises. These sounded as if they were running loose.'

'How do you know they were wolves? Did you actually see them?'

Childe admitted that he hadn't. Bruin said that even if there were laws against keeping wolves in that area, it would be the business of the Beverly Hills Police or perhaps the county police. He wasn't sure, because that area was doubtful; it was on the very edge of Beverly Hills, if he remembered right. He'd have to look it up.

Childe did not insist on finding out. He knew that Bruin was too busy to be interested and even if he wasn't busy he probably thought Childe was on a false trail. Childe admitted to himself that this was most likely. But he had nothing else to do.

The rest of the day he spent cleaning up his apartment, doing his washing in the apartment's basement machines, planning what he would do that evening, speculating, and collecting some material, which he put into his trunk.

He also watched the TV news. The air was as motionless and as grey as lead. Despite this, most of the citizens seemed to think that conditions were returning to normal. Businesses were open again, and cars were filling the streets. The authorities, however, had warned those who had left the area not to return if they had some place to stay. The 'unnatural' weather might continue indefinitely. There was no explanation for it which could be proved or even convincingly presented. But if normal atmospheric conditions did return, it would be best for those whose health was endangered by smog to stay away, or to plan on returning only long enough to settle their affairs before getting out.

Childe went to the supermarket, which was operating at almost one hundred percent normalcy, to stock up. The sky was greying swiftly, and the peculiar ghastly light had now spread over the sky from the horizon. It subdued the human beings under its dome; they spoke less frequently and more quietly and even the blaring of horns was reduced.

The birds had not returned.

Childe called Igescu twice. The first time, a recording said that all calls would be answered only after six. Childe wondered why the recorded call of the evening before had said he could phone in after three. Childe called again a few minutes after six. Magda Holyani's low voice answered.

Yes, Mr Igescu would see him at eight that evening. Sharp. And the interview would be over at nine. Mr Wellston would have to sign a paper which would require that any material to be published could be blue-lined by Mr Igescu. He could not bring a camera. The chauffeur, Eric Glam, would meet Mr Wellston at the gate and would drive him up. Mr Wellston's car would have to be parked outside the wall.

Childe had hung up and taken three steps from the phone when it rang. Bruin was calling. 'Childe, the report from the lab had been in for some time but I didn't have a chance to see it until a coupla minutes ago.'

He paused. Childe said, 'Well?'

'It was clean, just like Colben's car. Except for one thing.'

Bruin paused again. Childe felt a chill run over his back and then

63

up his neck and over his scalp. When he heard Bruin, he had the feeling of *déjà vu*, of having heard the words before under exactly identical circumstances. But it was not so much *déjà vu* as expectation.

'There were hairs on the front seat. Wolf hairs.'

'You've changed your mind about the possible worthwhileness of investigating Igescu?'

Bruin grunted and said, 'We can't. Not just now. But, yeah, I think you ought to. The wolf hairs were put on the seat on purpose, obviously, since everything else was so clean. Why? Who knows? I was looking for another film, this time about Budler, but we didn't get any in. So far.'

'It could be just a coincidence,' Childe said. 'But in case I don't report in to you by ten tonight, if it's OK for me to call your house, then you better call on the baron.'

'Hell, I probably won't be off duty by ten and no telling where I'll be. I could have your call relayed, but the lieutenant wouldn't like that, we're pretty tied up with official calls and this wouldn't rate as that. No, call Sergeant Mustanoja, he'll be on duty, and he'll take a message for me. I'll contact him when I get time.'

'Then let's make it eleven,' Childe said. 'Maybe I'll get hung up out there.'

'Not by the balls, I hope,' Bruin said, and laughing, clicked the phone.

Childe felt his testicles withdraw a little. He did not care much for Bruin's humour. Not while the film about Colben was still bright in his mind.

He took three paces, and the phone rang again. Magda Holyani said that she was sorry, but it was necessary that the interview be put off until nine.

Childe said that it would make little difference to him. Holyani said that that was nice and please make it nine *sharp*.

Childe called Bruin back to report the change in plans. Bruin was gone, so he left a note with Sergeant Mustanoja.

At 8.30 he drove out. From Beverly Boulevard, the hills appeared like ghosts too timorous or too weak as yet to clothe themselves with dense ectoplasm.

By the time he had pulled up before the gateway to the Igescu estate, night had settled. A big car inside the gate was pouring out light from its beams up the private road away from the gate.

A large form leaned against the gate. It turned, and the

64

extraordinarily broad-shouldered and lean-waisted figure of a giant was silhouetted against the lights. It wore a chauffeur's cap.

'I'm Mr Wellston. I have an appointment at nine.'

The voice sounded as if it were being pounded out on a big drum. 'Yes, sir. May I see your ID, sir?'

Childe produced several cards, a driver's licence, and a letter, all counterfeit. The chauffeur looked them over with the aid of a pencil-thin flashlight, handed them back through the opening in the gate, and walked off to one side. He disappeared behind the wall. The gate noiselessly swung inward. Childe walked in, and the gate swung back. Glam strode up, opened the rear door for him, and then shut it after Childe was in the back seat. He got into the driver's seat, and Childe could see that his ears were huge and at right angles to his head, seemingly as big as bats' wings. This was an exaggeration, of course, but they were enormous.

The drive was made in silence; the big Rolls-Royce swung back and forth effortlessly and without any noticeable motor noise. Its beams sprayed trees, firs, maples, oaks, and many thick bushes trimmed into various shapes. The light seemed to bring the vegetation into existence. After going perhaps half a mile as the crow flies, but two miles back and forth, the car stopped before another wall. This was of red brick, about nine feet high, and also had iron spikes with barbed wire between the spikes. Glam pressed something on the dashboard, and the gate's grille ironwork swung inward.

Childe looked through the windows but could see only more road and woods. Then, as the car came around the first bend, he saw the beams reflected against four gleaming eyes. The beams turned away, the eyes disappeared, but not before he had seen two wolfish shapes slinking off into the brush.

The car started up a steep hill and as it got near the top, its beams struck a Victorian cupola. The drive curved in front of the house and, as the beams swept across the building, Childe saw that it was, as the newspaper article had described it, rambling. The central part was obviously older and of adobe. The wings were of wood, painted grey, except for the red-trimmed windows, and they extended part way down the side of the hill, so that the house seemed to be like a huge octopus squatting on a rock.

This flashed across his mind, like a frame irrelevantly inserted in a reel, and then it became just a monstrous and incongruous building.

The original building had a broad porch and the added-on

buildings had also been equipped with porches. Most of the porch was in shadows, but the central portion was faintly illuminated with light leaking through thin blinds. A shadow passed across a blind and then was gone.

The car stopped. Glam lunged out and opened the door for Childe. Childe stood for a minute, listening. The wolves had not howled once. He wondered what was to keep them from attacking the people in the house. Glam did not seem worried about them.

'This way, sir,' Glam said and led him up the porch and to the front door. He pressed a button, and a light over the door came on. The door was of massive highly polished hardwood – mahogany? – carved to represent a scene from (it seemed likely) Hieronymus Bosch. But a closer look convinced him that the artist had been Spanish. There was something indefinably Iberian about the beings (demons, monsters, humans) undergoing various tortures or fornicating in some rather peculiar fashions with some rather peculiar organs.

Glam had left his chauffeur's cap on the front seat of the Rolls. He was dressed in a black flannel suit, and his trousers were stuffed into his boot-tops. He unlocked the door with a large key he produced from a pocket, swung the door open (it was well-oiled, no Inner-Sanctum squeaks), and bowed Childe on through. The room inside was a large (it could even be called great) hall. Two halls, rather, because one ran along the front of the house and halfway down it was a broad entrance to another hall which seemed to run the depth of the house. The carpets were thick and wine-coloured with a very faint pattern in green. A few pieces of heavy, solid Spanish-looking furniture sat against the walls.

Glam asked Childe to wait while he announced him. Childe watched the giant stoop to go through the doorway to the centre hall. Then he jerked his head to the right because he had caught a glimpse of somebody down at the far end just going around the corner. He was startled, because he had seen no one at that end when he came in. Now he saw the back of a tall woman, the floor-length full black skirt, white flesh of the back revealed in the V of the cut, high-piled black hair, a tall black comb.

He felt cold and, for a second, disoriented.

He had no more time to think about the woman then, because his host came to greet him. Igescu was a tall slim man with thick, wavy, brown-blond hair, large, bright green eyes, pointed features, a large curving nose, and a dimple in his right cheek. The moustache was

66

gone. He seemed to be about sixty-five years old, a vigorous athletic sixty-five. He wore a dark-blue business suit. His tie was black with a faint bluish symbol in its centre. Childe could not make it out; the outlines seemed to be fluid, to change shape as Igescu changed position.

His voice was deep and pleasant, and he spoke with only a tinge of foreign pronunciation. He shook hands with Childe. His hands were large and strong-looking and his grip was powerful. His hand was cold but not abnormally so. He was a very amiable and easy-going host but made it clear that he intended to allow his guest to remain only an hour. He asked Childe a few questions about his work and the magazine he represented. Childe gave him glib answers; he was prepared for more interrogation than he got.

Glam had disappeared somewhere. Igescu immediately took Childe on a guided tour. This lasted about five minutes and was confined to a few rooms on the first floor. Childe could not get much idea of the layout of the house. They returned to a large room off the central hall where Igescu asked Childe to sit down. This was also fitted with Spanish-type furniture and a grand piano. There was a fireplace, above the mantel of which was a large oil painting. Childe, sipping on an excellent brandy, listened to his host but studied the portrait. The subject was a beautiful young woman dressed in Spanish costume and holding a large ivory-yellowish fan. She had unusually heavy eyebrows and extremely dark eyes, as if the painter had invented a paint able to concentrate blackness. There was a faint smile about the lips – not Mona Lisaish, however – the smile seemed to indicate a determination to – what? Studying the lips, Childe thought that there was something nasty about the smile, as if there were a deep hatred there and a desire to get revenge. Perhaps the brandy and his surroundings made him think that or perhaps the artist was the nasty and hateful one and he had projected on to the innocent blankness of the subject his own feelings. Whatever the truth, the artist had talent. He had given the painting the authenticity of more than life.

He interrupted Igescu to ask him about the painting. Igescu did not seem annoyed.

'The artist's name was Krebens,' he said, 'If you get close to the painting, you'll see it in minuscule letters at the left-hand corner. I have a fairly good knowledge of art history and local history, but I have never seen another painting by him. The painting came with

67

the house; it is said to be of Dolores del Osorojo. I am convinced that it is, since I have seen the subject.'

He smiled. Childe felt cold again. He said, 'Just after I came in, I saw a woman going around the corner down the hall. She was dressed in old-fashioned Spanish clothes. Could that be . . ?'

Igescu said, 'There are only three women in this house. My secretary, my great-grandmother, and a house guest. None of them wear the clothing you describe.'

'The ghost seems to have been seen by quite a few people,' Childe said. 'You don't seem to be upset, however.'

Igescu shrugged and said, 'Three of us, Holyani, Glam, and I, have seen Dolores many times, although always at a distance and fleetingly. She is no illusion or delusion. But she seems harmless, and I find it easier to put up with her than with many flesh and blood people.'

'I wish you had permitted me to bring a camera. This house is very colourful, and if I could have caught her on film . . . or have you tried that and found out she doesn't photograph?'

'She didn't when I first moved in,' Igescu said. 'But I caught her a year ago and the developed film showed her quite clearly. The furniture behind her showed dimly, but she's much more opaque than she used to be. Given time, and enough people to feed off . . .'

He waved his hand as if that would complete the sentence. Childe wondered if Igescu were putting him on. He said, 'Could I see that photo?'

'Certainly,' Igescu said. 'But it won't prove anything, of course. There is very little that can't be faked.'

He spoke into an intercom disguised as a cigar humidor in a language Childe did not recognize. It certainly did not sound Latin, although, unacquainted with Rumanian, he had no way of identifying it. He doubted that Rumanian would have such back-of-the-throat sounds.

He heard the click of billiard balls, and turned to look down into the next room. Two people were playing. They were both blond, of medium height, well built, and clothed in tight-fitting white sweaters, tight-fitting white jeans, and black sandals. They looked as if they could be brother and sister. Their eyebrows were high and arched and the eye sockets were deep. Their lips were peculiar. The upper lip was so thin it looked like the edge of a bloody knife; the lower lip was so swollen that it looked as if it had been cut and infected by the upper.

Igescu called to them. They raised their heads with such a lupine air that Childe could not help thinking of the wolves he had glimpsed on the way up. They nodded at Childe when Igescu introduced them as Vasili Chornkin and Mrs Krautschner but they did not smile or say anything. They seemed eager to get back to their game. Igescu did not explain what their status was but Childe thought that the girl must be the house guest he had mentioned.

Glam appeared suddenly and noiselessly, as if he slid spaces around him instead of moving himself. He gave a manila envelope to Igescu. Childe glanced at Igescu as he removed the photo from the envelope, then he looked up. Glam had gone as swiftly and silently as he had entered.

The photo was taken from about forty feet during the daytime. Light flooding in from the large window showed everything in detail. There was Dolores del Osorojo just about to leave the hall through a doorway. The edge of the doorway and part of a chair nearby could be faintly made out through her. She was looking back at the camera with the same faint smile as in her painting.

'I'll have to have it back,' Igescu said.

10

'As you say, a photo proves nothing,' Childe said. He looked at his wristwatch. A half hour left. He opened his mouth to ask about the car accident and the morgue incident but Magda Holyani entered.

She was a tall, slim, small-breasted woman of about thirty with beautiful although disproportioned features and thick pale-yellow hair. She walked as if her bones were flexible or as if her flesh encased ten thousand delicate intricately articulated bones. The bones of her head seemed to be thin; her cheekbones were high, and her eyes were tilted. The mouth was too thin. There was something indefinably reptilian about her, or, to be more exact, snakish. This was not repulsive. After all, many snakes are beautiful.

Her eyes were so light he thought at first they were colourless, but, closer, they became a very light grey. Her skin was very white, as if she shunned not only the sun but the day. It was, however, flawless. She had no make-up whatever. The lips would have looked pale if she had been standing next to a woman with rouged lips, but set against her own white skin they seemed dark and bright.

She wore a tight-fitting black dress with a deep square-cut bodice and almost no back. Her stockings were black nylon, and the high-heeled shoes were black. She sat down after being introduced, revealing beautiful, but seemingly boneless, legs from the mid-thigh down. She took over the conversation from Igescu, who lit up an expensive cigar and seemed to become lost in gazing into the smoke.

Childe tried to keep the conversation to a question-and answer interview, but she replied briefly and unsatisfactorily and followed with a question each time about himself or his work. He felt that *he* was being interviewed.

He was becoming desperate. This would be his only chance to find out anything, and he was not even getting a 'feel' of rightness or wrongness about this place and its tenants. They were a little odd, but this meant nothing, especially in Southern California.

He noticed that Glam was busying himself nearby with emptying the Baron's and Magda's ash trays, refilling the glasses, and at the same time managing to keep his eyes on the woman. Once, he touched her, and she snapped her head back and glared at him. Igescu was aware that Childe was taking this in, but he only smiled.

Finally, Childe ignored her to ask Igescu directly if he would care to comment on the much-publicized 'vampire' incident. After all, it was this that had brought him out here. And so far he had not learned much. The article would be spare, if indeed he had enough data to make an article.

'Frankly, Mr Wellston,' Igescu said, 'I permitted this interview because I wanted to kill people's curiosity about this once and for all. Essentially, I am a man who likes privacy; I am wealthy but I leave the conduct of my business to others and enjoy myself. You have seen my library. It is very extensive and expensive and contains many first editions. It covers a wide variety of subjects. I can say without bragging that I am an extremely well-read man in many languages. Ten shelves are filled with books on my hobby: precious stones. But you may also have observed several shelves filled with books on such subjects as witchcraft, vampirism, lycanthropy, and so on. I am somewhat interested in these, but not, Mr Wellston, because I take a professional interest.'

He smiled over his cigar and said, 'No, it is not because I am a vampire, Mr Wellston, that I have read in these subjects. I took no interest in them until after the incident that caused you to come here. I thought that if I were to be accused of being a vampire, I had better find out just what a vampire was. I knew something about them, of course, because, after all, I do come from the Carpathians and from an area in which the peasants believe more in vampires and the devil than they do in God. But my tutors never went much into folk-lore, and my contacts with the local non-nobility were not intimate.

'I decided to give you this interview so that, once and for all, this nonsense about my vampirism could be quelled. And also, to divert attention from me towards the only truly supernatural feature of this house: Dolores del Osorojo. I have changed my mind about photographs for your article. I will have Magda send you a number. These will show some of the rooms in the house and various photos of the ghost. I will do this on the condition that you make it clear in your article that I am a man who likes privacy and a quiet life and that the vampire talk is nonsense. After getting that out of the way, you may stress the ghost as much as you like. But you must also make it clear that there will be no other interviews with anybody and that I do not like to be disturbed by curiosity-seekers, eccentric spiritualists or journalists. Agreed?'

'Certainly, Mr Igescu. You have my word. And of course, as

agreed, you will edit the article before it's published.'

Childe felt a little dizzy. He wished that he had not accepted the brandy. It had been four years since he had drunk anything, and he would not have broken his rule now, except that Igescu had praised the brandy as being so rare that he had been tempted to try it. And he had also not wanted to offend his host in any way if he could help it. He had, however, not had more than one tumbler. The stuff was either very potent or he was vulnerable after the long dry period.

Igescu turned his head to look at the tall dark grandfather clock. 'Your time is about up, Mr Wellston.'

Childe wondered why the baron was so concerned with time, when, by his own admission, he seldom went any place or did anything particularly pressing. But he did not ask. The baron would have regarded such a question as too impertinent to answer with anything but cold silence.

Igescu stood up. Childe rose also. Magda Holyani finished her drink and got up from the chair. Glam appeared in the doorway, but Igescu said, 'Miss Holyani will drive Mr Wellston to the gate, Glam. I need you for another duty.'

Glam opened his mouth as if he meant to object but shut it immediately. He said, 'Very well, sir,' and wheeled around and walked away.

Igescu said, 'If you'd like some more material for your article, Mr Wellston, you might look up Michel Le Garrault in the UCLA library. I have copies of two of his works, first editions, by the way. The old Belgian had some very interesting and original theories about vampires, werewolves, and other so-called supernatural phenomena. His theory of *psychic imprinting* is fascinating. Have you read him? Can you read French?'

'Never heard of him,' Childe said, wondering if he would have fallen into a trap if he had professed familiarity. 'I do read French.'

'There are many so-called authorities on the occult and supernatural who have not heard of Le Garrault or had no chance to read him. I recommend that you go to the rare book section of the UCLA library and ask for *Les Murs S'écroulés*. Translations of the original Latin were made in French, and curiously, in Bohemian, and these are very rare indeed. There are, as far as I know, only ten Latin copies in the world. The Vatican has one; a Swedish monastery has two; I have one; the Kaiser of Germany had one but it was lost or, probably, stolen after he died at Doorn; and the other five are in state

72

libraries at Moscow, Paris, Washington, London, and Edinburgh.'

'I'll look him up,' Childe said. 'Thanks very much for the information.'

He turned to follow Igescu out and saw the woman in Spanish dress, high comb stuck in her black hair, just stepping into a doorway at the end of the hall. She turned her head and smiled and then was gone.

Igescu said, calmly, 'Did you see her, too?'

'Yes, I did. But I couldn't see through her,' Childe said.

'I did,' Magda Holyani said. Her voice shook a little. Childe looked at her. She seemed to be angry, not frightened.

'As I said, she has been getting more and more opaque,' Igescu said. 'The solidifying is so subtle, that it's only noticeable if you compare what she was six months ago with what she now is. The process has been very slow but steady. When I first moved in here, she was almost invisible.'

Childe shook his head. Was he really discussing a ghost as if it existed? And why was Magda so upset? She had stopped and was staring at the doorway as if she were resisting the impulse to chase off after the thing.

'Many people, more people than care to admit, have seen ghostly phenomena – something weird and unexplainable, anyway – but either the phenomenon doesn't repeat itself or else the people "visited" ignore it and it goes away. But Dolores, ah, there is another story! Dolores is ignored by me, except for an occasional picture-taking. Magda used to ignore her but now she seems to be getting on her nerves. Dolores is gaining substance from somewhere, perhaps from someone in this house.'

Certainly, the story of Dolores was gaining substance. If a photo of her was no evidence that she existed, neither was the fact that he had seen her. For some reason, Igescu might have planned this whole thing, and if he, Childe, were to run after Dolores and try to seize her, what would his hands close on? He had a feeling that he would grip solid flesh and that the young woman would turn out to have come into existence about twenty years ago, not one hundred and fifty.

At the door, he shook hands with Igescu, thanked him, and promised to send him a carbon of the article for editing. He followed Magda to the car and turned once before getting in to look back. Igescu was gone, but a blind had been half-raised and Glam's bulldog face and batwing ears were plainly visible.

He got into the front seat with Magda, at her invitation. She said, 'My job pays very well, you know. It has to. It's the only thing that would make it endurable. I almost never get a chance to go to town and the only ones I can talk to, ever, are my boss and a few servants and occasionally a guest.'

'Is it hard work?' Childe asked, wondering why she was telling him this. Perhaps she had to unburden herself to someone.

'No. I take care of his few social obligations, make appointments, act as middle man between him and his business managers, do some typing on the book he's writing on jewels, and spend more time than I care to staying away from that monster, Glam.'

'He did nothing definite, but I got the idea that he's quite attached to you,' Childe said.

The beams swept across trees as the car went around a corner. The moon was up now, and he could see more distinctly. He could be wrong, but it seemed to him that they were not on the same road he had travelled on the way up.

'I'm taking the longer, no less scenic, route,' she said, as if she had read his mind. 'I hope you don't mind. I feel that I just have to talk to somebody. You don't have to listen to me, of course, there's no reason why you should.'

'Pour it on me,' he said. 'I like to hear your voice.'

They passed through the gateway of the inner wall. She drove slowly, in first gear, as she talked, and once she put her hand on his leg. He did not move. She took her hand off after a minute when she had to stop the car. They had driven off the road on to a narrow stone-covered path which led through a break in the trees to a clearing. A small summerhouse, a rough wooden structure on a high round cement base, stood there. Its open sides were partially covered with vines, so that its interior was dark. A flight of cement steps led up to the wide entrance.

'I get very lonely,' she said, 'although the baron is charming and does talk a lot. But he's not interested in me in the way some employers are in their female employees.'

He did not have to ask her what she meant by that. She had put her hand on his leg again, seemingly as accidentally or unselfconsciously as before. He said, 'Are there wolves out here, too? Or are they all inside the inner wall?'

She was leaning closer now, and her perfume was so strong that it seemed to soak into his pores. He felt his penis swelling and he took her hand and moved it so that it was on his penis. She did not try to take her hand away.

He reached over and ran a finger down along the curve of the left breast and down the cleavage into the breast. His hand went on down and slid between the cloth and breast and rubbed over the nipple. The nipple swelled, and she shuddered. He kissed her with many slidings of his tongue along hers and over her teeth. She fumbled along his zipper, found it, pulled it slowly down, and then probed through the openings of his jockey shorts. He unbuttoned the front of her dress and quickly verified what he had suspected. She wore nothing beneath the dress except for a narrow suspender belt. The breasts were small but shapely and were swelling with blood. He bent over and took a nipple in his mouth and began sucking. She was breathing as hard as he.

'Let's go in the summerhouse,' she said softly. 'There's a couch in there.'

'All right,' he said. 'But before we go any further, you should know I'm unprepared. I don't have any rubbers.'

He would not have been surprised if she'd said that she had some in her handbag. It wouldn't have been the first time that this had happened to him.

But she said, 'Never mind. I won't get pregnant.'

Shakily, he followed her out of the car, sliding past the wheel. She turned and slid the dress off her shoulders. The moonlight gleamed on the whitest flesh possible, on dark wet nipples, and dark triangle of pubic hairs below the suspender belt. She kicked her shoes off and, clad only in belt and stockings, swayed towards the summerhouse.

He followed her, but he was not so excited that he did not wonder about cameras and sound devices in the summerhouse. He knew that he was good-looking, but he was not, after all, a god who swept all women before him on a tide of desire. If Magda Holyani seduced him on such short acquaintance, she either was very hard-up or had a motive that he might not like if he knew. Or possibly, both. She did not seem to be faking her passion.

If, for some reason, she thought she could lead him so far, turn him on and then turn him off, she was going to be surprised. He had suffered a good part of yesterday with a painful ball-ache because of his unfinished love-making with Sybil, and he did not intend to suffer again.

Inside the house, he looked around. There could be no cameras hidden here. If there were any, they'd have to be attached to the trees on the edge of the clearing, and he could not see how they would be able to film much, even if they were equipped with black-light devices. The vines and their supports would bar anything except patches of skin and an occasional glimpse of a head or limb. Besides, what did he have to lose? Blackmail could not be the object of such a game.

Magda yanked off the blanket acting as a dust cover for the sofa. She turned then, the moonlight falling through the vines dappling her pale skin. Childe took her in his arms and kissed her again, ran his hands down her back, feeling the hard muscles – she had the muscle tone of a young puma – the inward fall of the waist and the outward fall of the hips. The suspender belt annoyed him, so he sank to his knees and unfastened the stockings and pulled them down and then pulled down on the belt. She kicked them to one side and put her hands on the back of his head and pulled him towards her cunt. He allowed her to press his face against the hairs, and ran his tongue out and inserted it just below the opening of the lips and tickled her clitoris with its tip. She moaned and clutched him tighter.

But he stood up, sliding his tongue up from her cunt and along her belly and up to her nipple, which he began to suck again. He stepped her backwards until she fell on the sofa, her legs sticking out, her heels resting on the floor. Then he got down on his knees again and licked her clitoris once more and then slid down and thrust his tongue again and again into her vagina. She began to twist her hips a little, but he reached up and pressed down on her belly to indicate that she should hold still.

Her cunt tasted as sweet as Sybil's, and the hairs seemed to be softer. He put one finger inside her cunt and another finger of the same hand up her anus and then, working the hand slowly in and out, rubbed his tongue back and forth over her clitoris and then later tongue-fucked her while his fingers increased the speed of their in-and-out into her cunt and anus.

She came with a scream and a sudden tightening of thighs about his head. The grip was so strong that he could not move his fingers.

He could stand it no longer. He had had no emissions for two weeks because of involvement in a case which he had wound up just before Colben disappeared. He had been busy night and day and when he managed to snatch some sleep even his unconscious had been too tired to whip up a sexual dream. Then the frustrations with Sybil had made him hypersensitive. In a minute, he was going to come, whether he was in Magda or the air.

'I can't wait,' he said. 'It's been too long.'

He started to get down beside her and to help her scoot up on the sofa so she could lie full length. But she said, 'You're ready to come?'

'It's been too long. I'm full to bursting,' he groaned.

She pushed him down and ran her tongue along his belly and wet his pubic hairs with her saliva and tongue and then closed her lips upon the head of his cock. She slid it back and forth in her lips twice, and with a scream that matched hers of a moment ago, he burst in her mouth.

He lay there, feeling as if a tide inside him were withdrawing to some far-off horizon. He did not say anything; he expected her to get up and spit out the stuff, as Sybil always did. Sybil also always immediately brushed her teeth and gargled with Listerine. Not that he blamed her, certainly. He could understand that, once the excitement was gone, the thick ropy stuff could become disgusting. He knew how it tasted. When he had been fourteen, he and his fifteen-year-old brother had gone through a period of about six months when they had sucked each other off. And then, by mutual and silent consent, they had quit and that had been the last of his homosexual experiences and, as far as he knew, of his brother's. Certainly, his brother, who was such a cocksman that he must be a compulsive, hated fairies, and once, many years later, when Childe had referred to their experimentations, his brother had not known what he was talking about. He was either too ashamed of it now to admit it or else had actually buried it so deep that he did not remember.

But Magda did not leave him. She audibly swallowed several times and then renewed her sucking. He sat up and bent over so he could cup her breasts in his hands while she was mouthing his glans. And then, just as his penis was at almost full erection, he thought of Colben and the iron teeth. This woman could be the actress in that movie.

She looked up at him suddenly and said, 'What's wrong?'

'Listen,' he said, 'and don't get mad. Or laugh. But do you have false teeth?'

She sat up and said, 'What?' Her voice was thick with fluid.

'Do you have false teeth?'

'Why do you want to know?' Then she laughed and said, 'You

want me to take them out?'

'If you have false teeth.'

'Do I look that old?'

'I've known several nineteen-year-olds who had choppers,' he said.

'Kiss me and I'll tell you,' she said.

'Certainly.'

He held her tightly while he probed her mouth with his tongue. He sniffed the wild-beast odour of his own semen and tasted the thick-oil gluey-seeming product of his own body. Far from being unpleasant, it excited him. She had her hand on his cock, and, feeling it swell, immediately withdrew from his arms and went down on him again. Evidently, she did not intend for him to find out if she did have false teeth or perhaps she thought that his tongue would have determined that.

Whatever her reasons, she would not tell him, unless he were to use force, he was sure of that. He leaned back and let her work on him. And after a while he rolled her over and she opened her legs and took his penis gently in her fingers and guided him in. He had no sooner sunk in to the hairs than she squeezed down on his cock with her muscles and continued to squeeze as if she had a hand inside her cunt. And then, once again, thinking of the film, he became soft. He remembered that bulge behind the G-string of the woman in the film.

'For God's sake,' she said. 'What's the matter now?'

'I thought I saw somebody in the shadows,' he said, the only excuse he could grasp at the moment. 'Glam?'

'It had better not be,' she said. 'I'll kill him if it is. So will the baron.'

She stood up on the sofa and called, 'Glam? Glam? If you're there, you asshole, you better start running and fast. Otherwise, it's the other end of the wolf for you.'

There was no answer. Childe said, 'The other end of the wolf? What do you mean?'

'I'll tell you later,' she said. 'He's not out there; if he is, he isn't going to bother us. Come on, please. I'm ready to explode.'

Instead of reaching for him, she got down off the sofa and crossed the summerhouse to a small cabinet on a stand in the shadows. She came back with a bottle with a squat body and a long narrow neck with a wide mouth. It was half-full. She drank some, swished some in her mouth, and still holding it, pressed her lips against his and squirted the liquid into his mouth. It was hot and thick and slightly

78

tart. He swallowed some and immediately felt his anxieties draining off.

'What the hell is that?'

'It's a liqueur made in Igescu's native province,' she said. 'It's supposed to have an aphrodisiac effect. I understand that there isn't any true aphrodisiac, but this stuff does one thing. It burns away the inhibitions. Not that I thought I'd ever have to use it on you.'

'I won't need any more of it,' he said. His penis was rising as if it were a balloon being filled for a transatlantic voyage. A beam of moonlight fell on it, and Magda, seeing it, squealed with delight.

'Oh, you beauty! You great big beauty!'

She lay down and raised her legs and he entered again and then, for a long time, said nothing. It was a peculiarity of his that if he were blown at the beginning, he took a long time coming the second time. Magda seemed to have an almost unbroken series of orgasms during this time and when he finally came she clawed his back until the blood ran off. He did not mind at the time, but later he cursed her. It was a theory of his that women who clawed your back when they came were actually attempting to prove how passionate they were, but he was willing to admit that he could be wrong.

They lay there for some time by each other, not saying a word. They were sheathed in sweat and would have been grateful for a breeze. But the air was as still as before.

Finally, he said, 'There's no use your playing with it. Not for some time. I'm shot out. I could stay and be all right within an hour, but I have to go pretty soon.'

He was thinking that he was supposed to have called Mustanoja by now.

'I'm not unsatisfied, baby,' she said, 'but I could be whipped up into enthusiasm again, and I'd like to be. You don't know how long it's been for me!'

She reached for the bottle, which was on the floor by the sofa.

'Let's have another drink and see what happens.'

He watched her to make sure that she drank again out of the bottle before he drank. He took a small swallow and then said, 'What's this about Glam and the other end of the wolf?'

She laughed and said, 'That big ugly dumbshit! He wants me, but I can't stand him, and he'd probably try to rape me, he's such a moron, but he knows that if I didn't kill him, Igescu would! You must know about the wolves, since you mentioned them. I was walking in

79

the woods one evening when I heard one of the wolves howling and snarling. It sounded as if it were in pain, or, at least, in trouble of some kind. I went up a hill and looked down in a hollow, and there was the female wolf, her head in four nooses, and the ends of the nooses tied to trees. She couldn't go back or forward, and there was Glam, all his clothes off except for his socks and shoes, holding the wolf by the tail and fucking her. I think he must have been hurting her, I don't know how big a female wolf's cunt is, but I don't think they're built to take an enormous cock like Glam's. I really think she was hurt. But Glam, that animal Glam, was fucking her.'

Childe was silent for a moment and then he said, 'What about the male wolf? Wasn't Glam afraid of the male wolf?'

She laughed and said, 'Oh, that's another story,' and she laughed for a long time.

When she stopped, she raised the bottle and poured liquid on her nipples and then on her pubic hairs.

'Lick it off, baby, and then we'll make love again.'

'It won't do any good,' Childe said. But he rolled over and sucked on her nipples for a while and fingerfucked her until she came again and again and then he kissed her belly, travelling downward until his mouth was against the tight hairs of her cunt. He tongued off the liqueur and then jabbed his tongue as far as he could until his jaws and tongue hurt. When he stopped, he was rolled over by her strong hands and she gently nibbled at his penis until it rose like a trout to a fly. This time, he mounted her from behind, and she told him to be quiet, he did not have to wear himself out. She contracted the muscles of her vagina as if it were a hand and this time he kept his erection. He seemed to be getting a little dizzy and a little fuzzy. He knew that he had made a mistake drinking that liquid; it couldn't be poison, because she wouldn't have drunk it also. But he wondered if it had a property of becoming narcotic if it were on epidermis. Could its interaction with the skin of her nipples and cunt have produced something dangerous only to him?

Then the thought and the alarm were gone.

He remembered vaguely an orgasm that seemed to go on forever, like the thousand-year orgasm promised the faithful of Islam in heaven when they are enfolded by an houri. There were blanks thereafter. He could remember, as if he were seeing himself in a fog, getting his car and driving off while the road wiggled like a snake and the trees bent over and made passes at him with their branches. Some of the trees seemed to have big knotty eyes and mouths like barky cunts. The eyes became nipples; sap oozed out of them. A tree gave him the finger with the end of a branch.

'Up yours, too,' he remembered yelling, and then he was on a broad road with many lights around him and horns blaring and then there was the same tree again and this time it beckoned at him and as he got closer he could see that its mouth *was* a barky cunt and that it was promising him something he had never had before.

And so it was. Death.

11

He awoke in the emergency room of the Doctors Hospital in Beverly Hills. His only complaint was sluggishness. He was unconscious when he had been pulled out of the car by a good Samaritan. The Beverly Hills officer told him that his car had run into a tree off the side of the road, but the collision was so light that the only damage was a slightly bent-in bumper and a broken headlamp.

The officer evidently suspected first, drunkenness, and second, drugs. Childe told him that he had been forced off the road and had been knocked out when the car hit the tree. That he had no visible injury on his head meant nothing.

Fortunately, there were no witnesses to the crash. The man who had pulled him from the car had come around the curve just in time to see the impact. Another car was going in the opposite direction; it was not driving erratically, as Childe had reported, but this meant nothing because the car could have straightened out. Childe gave Bruin and several others as references. Fifteen minutes later, he was discharged, although the doctors warned him that he should take it easy even if there was no evidence of concussion.

His car was still on the roadside. The police had not had it towed in because the trucks were too busy, but the officer had removed the key from the ignition. Unfortunately, the officer had also forgotten to give it back to Childe, and Childe then had to walk to the Beverly Hills Police Department to retrieve it. The officer was on duty. A radio call resulted in the information that he was tied up and would not be able to drop by the department for at least an hour. Childe made sure that the key would be given to the officer in charge of the desk, and he walked home through the night. He cursed himself for having buried the extra key under the bush outside Igescu's and then forgetting to dig it up again.

He had tried to get a taxi to take him home, but these were too busy. It seemed that everybody thought that the smog was over for good and was celebrating. Or perhaps everybody wanted to have some fun before the air became too poisoned again.

There were three parties going on in his building. He put ear plugs in as soon as he had showered, and went to bed. The plugs kept most of the noise out but did not help bar his thoughts.

He had been drugged and sent out with the hope that he would kill himself in a car accident. Why the drug had affected him and not Magda was an interesting question but one that did not have to be considered at this time. She could have taken an antidote or relied on someone else to take care of her after Childe was gone. Or it was possible – he remembered what he had thought during the time – that the liquid contained something which did not become a drug unless it contacted human exterior epidermis?

He sat up in bed then. Sergeant Mustanoja! He should have been worrying about Childe's failure to call in. What had he done – if anything?

He phoned the LAPD and got Mustanoja. Yeah, he had the note but Bruin didn't seem to think it was important and, anyway, what with being so busy – what a night! – he had forgotten it. That is, until this Beverly Hills officer called in about him and then Mustanoja had found out what happened and knew he was not at Igescu's so what was there to worry about, huh? How was Childe?

Childe said he was home and OK. He hung up with some anger at Bruin for making light of his concern. However, he had to admit that there was no reason for Bruin to do otherwise. He would change his opinion after he found out what had happened last night. Perhaps, Bruin could arrange with the Beverly Hills Police Department . . . No, that wasn't going to work. The BHPD had far more immediate duties than investigating what was, objectively speaking, a very hazy lead. And there were certain things, important things, about the events that Childe was not going to tell them. He could skip the summerhouse activities and just say that he had been drugged with the brandy in the drawing room, but the officers were shrewd, they had known so many false tales and part-true tales, so many omissions and hesitations, that they picked up untruths and distortions as easily as radar distinguished an eagle from an airliner.

Besides, he had the feeling that Magda would not hesitate to claim that Childe had raped her and forced 'perversions' upon her.

He had got into bed again but now he climbed out swiftly once more. He felt ashamed and sick. That drug had overcome his normal fastidiousness and caution. He would never have gone down on a woman he just met. He always reserved this act – even if he were strongly tempted to do it – for women whom he knew well, liked or loved, and was reasonably sure were free from syphilis or gonorrhoea.

Although he had brushed his teeth, he went into the bathroom and brushed them again and then gargled deeply ten times with a burning mouthwash. From the kitchen cabinet he took a bottle of bourbon, which he kept for guests, and drank it straight. It was a dumb act, because he doubted that the alcohol would kill any germs he had swallowed so many hours ago, but it, like many purely ritual acts, made him feel better and cleaner.

He started for bed again and then stopped. He had been so upset that he had forgotten to check in with the exchange or turn on the recorder. He tried the exchange and hung up after the phone rang thirty times. Apparently, the exchange was not yet operating again or had lost its third-shift operator. The recorder yielded one call. It was from Sybil, at nine o'clock. She asked him to please call her as soon as he came in, no matter what time it was.

It was now three-ten in the morning.

Her phone rang uninterruptedly. The ring seemed to him like the tolling of a faraway bell. He envisioned her lying on the bed, one hand drooping over the edge of the bed, her mouth open, the eyes open and glazed. On the little table by the bed was an empty bottle of phenobarbitol.

If she had tried to kill herself again, she would be dead by now. That is, if she had taken the same amount as the last time.

He had sworn that if she tried again, she would have to go through with it, at least as far as he was concerned.

Nevertheless, he dressed and was out on the street and walking within a minute. He arrived at her apartment panting, his eyes burning, his lungs doubly burned from exertion and smog. The poison was accumulating swiftly, so swiftly that by tomorrow evening it would be as thick as before – unless the winds came.

Her apartment was silent. His heart was beating and his stomach clenching as he entered her bedroom and switched on the light. Her bed was not only empty, it had not been slept in. And her suitcases were gone.

He went over the apartment carefully but could find nothing to indicate 'foul play'. Either she had gone on a trip or someone had taken the suitcases so that that impression would be given.

If she had wanted him to know that she was leaving, why hadn't she left the message?

Perhaps her call and her sudden departure were unrelated.

There was the possibility that they were directly related but that she had told him only enough to get him over here so that he would worry about her. She could be angry enough to want to punish him. She had been mean enough to do similar things. But she had always quickly relented and tearfully and shamefully called him.

He sat down in an easy chair, then got up again and went into the kitchen and opened the *secret* compartment in the wall of the cabinet rear, second shelf up. The little round candy cup and its contents of white-paper-wrapped marijuana sticks – fifteen in all – were still there.

If she had left willingly, she would have disposed of this first.

Unless she were very upset.

He had not found her address book in any of the drawers when he had searched, but he looked again to make sure. The book was not there, and he doubted that any of the friends she had when they were married would know her whereabouts. She had been dropped by them or she had dropped them after the divorce. There was one, a life-long friend, whom she still wrote to now and then, but she had moved from California over a year ago.

Perhaps her mother was ill, and Sybil had left in a hurry. But she wouldn't be in such a hurry that she wouldn't have left the message with the recorder.

He did not remember her mother's number but he knew her address. He got the information from the operator and put a call through to the San Francisco address. The phone rang for a long time. Finally, he hung up and then thought of what he should have immediately checked. He was deeply upset to have overlooked that.

He went into the basement garage. Her car was still there.

By then he was considering the fantastic – or was it fantastic – possibility that Igescu had taken her.

First, why would Igescu do this?

If Igescu had been responsible for Colben's death and Budler's disappearance, then he might have designs on the detective investigating the case. Childe had pretended to be Wellston, the magazine reporter, but he had been forced to give his own phone number. And Igescu might have checked out the so-called Wellston. Certainly, Igescu had the money to do this.

What if Igescu had found out that Wellston was really Childe? And, having found out that Childe had not got into the serious car accident he had hoped for, he had taken Sybil away. Perhaps Igescu planned to let Childe know that he had better drop the investigation . . . no, it would be more probably that Igescu wanted to force him to break into the estate, to trespass. For reasons of his own, of course.

Childe shook his head. If Igescu were guilty, if he, say, had been guilty of other crimes, why was he suddenly letting the police know that these crimes had been committed?

This question was not one to be answered immediately. The only thing as of this moment was whether or not Sybil had gone voluntarily and, if she had not, with whom had she gone?

He had not checked the airports. He sat down and began dialling. The phones of every airline were busy, but he hung on until he got through to each and then went through more exasperating waits while passenger lists were checked. At the end of two hours, he knew that she had not taken a plane out. She might have intended to, but the airlines had been overburdened ever since the smog had become serious. The waiting lists were staggeringly long, and the facilities at the ports, the restaurants and toilets, had long queues. Parking facilities no longer existed for newcomers. Too many people had simply left their cars and taken off with no intention of returning immediately. The authorities had imposed an emergency time limitation, but the process of towing away cars to make room for others was tedious, involved, and slow. The traffic jam-up around International Airport demanded more police officers than were available.

He ate some cereal and milk and then, though it hurt him to think of all the money wasted, he flushed the marijuana down the toilet. If she continued to be missing and he had to notify the police, her apartment would be searched. On the other hand, if she were to return soon and find her supply gone, she would be in a rage. But surely she would understand why he had had to get rid of the stuff.

Dawn had arrived by then. The sun was a twisted pale-yellow thing in the sky. Visibility was limited to a hundred feet. The eye-burning and the nostril-scorching and the lung-searing were back.

He decided to call Bruin and to tell him about Sybil. Bruin would, of course, think that he was being unduly concerned and would think, even if he didn't say so, that she had simply left for an extended shacking-up with some man. Or, possibly, Bruin being the cynic he was, she was shacking up with some woman.

He did not have to phone Bruin. Bruin called him as he stood before the phone.

'We got a package in the late mail yesterday afternoon but it wasn't opened until a little while ago. You better get down here, Childe. Can you make it in half an hour?'

'What's it about? Budler?' And then, 'Never mind. But how did you know I was here?'

'I tried your place and you didn't answer, so I thought I'd try your ex-wife's. I knew you was still friendly with her.'

'Yeah,' Childe said, realizing that it was too early to report her missing. 'I'll be down in time. See you. Unh-unh! Maybe I can't! I have to get my car first and that may take some time.'

He told Bruin what had happened but censored the summerhouse activities. Bruin was silent for a long time and then said, 'You realize, Childe, that we're all doing a juggling act now, keeping three balls or more in the air at the same time? I'd investigate Igescu even if you don't have anything tangible or provable, because they sure sound like a fishy lot, but I doubt we could get into that place without a court order and we don't have any evidence to get an order. You know that. So it's up to you. Those wolf hair's in Budler's car and now this film – well, I ain't going to tell you about it, you got to see it to believe it – but if you can't get down here on time . . . listen, I could have a squad car pick you up. I would if this was ordinary times, but there's none available. Tell you what, if I'm out, you can get the film run off again, I'll leave word it's OK. Anyway, it might be shown again for the Commissioner. He's up to his ass in work, but he's taking a special interest in this case, and no wonder.'

Childe drank some orange juice, shaved (Sybil kept a man's razor and shaving cream for him and – he suspected – for other men) and then walked to the Beverly Hills Police Department. He got his key from the desk sergeant and asked if it were possible to get a ride with a squad car out to his car. He was told it was not possible. He tried to get a taxi, could not, and decided to hitchhike out. After fifteen minutes, he gave up. There were not many autos on Santa Monica Boulevard and Rexford, and the few that did go by ignored him. He did not blame them. Picking up hitchhikers at any time was potentially dangerous, but in this eerie white-lighted smog anybody would have looked sinister. Moreover, the radio, TV, and newspapers were advising caution because of the number of crimes in the streets.

His eyes teary and the interior of his nostrils and throat feeling as if he were sniffing in fumes from boiling metal, he stood upon the corner. He could see the house across the street and make out the city hall and the public library across the street from it as dim bulks, motionless icebergs in a fog. Far down, or seemingly far down, Rexford Avenue, a pair of headlights appeared and then swung out of sight.

Presently a black-and-white squad car passed him. When it was almost out of sight up Rexford, it stopped and then backed up until it was by him. The officer on the right, without getting out of the car, asked him what he was doing there. Childe told him. Fortunately, the officer had heard about him. He invited Childe to get in and ride with them. They had no definite goal at that moment; they were cruising around the area (the wealthy residential district, of course) but there was nothing to stop them from going that far out. Childe had to understand that if they got a call, they might have to dump him out on the spot and he would be stranded again. Childe said that he would take a chance.

It took fifteen minutes to get to his car. Only an emergency would have forced them to speed through this thick milky stuff. He thanked them and then started the car without any trouble, backed up, and swung towards town. Forty minutes later, he was parked in the LAPD visitors' lot.

12

Budler was in the same room in which Colben had been killed. The first scenes had shown Budler being conditioned, going through fear and impotence at first and then confidence and active, eager participation. In the beginning, he had been strapped to the same table but later the table was gone and a bed took its place.

Budler was a little man with narrow shoulders and skinny hips and legs, but he had a tremendous penis. He was pale-skinned and had light blue eyes and straw-coloured hair on his head. His pubic hairs were a light brown. His penis, however, was dark, as if blood always filled it. He had an unusual capacity for sustaining erections after orgasms and an unusual supply of seminal fluid.

(Both victims had been men with hypersex drives, or, at least, men whose lives seemed to be dominated by sex. Both were promiscuous, both had made a number of girls pregnant, been arrested or suspected of statutory rape, and were known as loudmouths about their conquests. Both were what his wife described as 'creeps'. There was something nasty about them. Childe thought that the victims had possibly been selected with poetic justice in mind.)

The woman with the garish make-up, and the creature? – machine? organ? – concealed behind her G-string, was an actor; she specialized in sucking cock and she took out her teeth several times but she did not use the iron teeth. Every time he saw her remove the false teeth, Childe tensed and felt sick but he was spared the mutilation.

There were other actors, also. One was an enormously fat woman with beautiful white skin. Her face never appeared. There was another woman, whose figure was superb, whose face was always hidden, usually by a mask. Both of these used their mouths and cunts, and once Budler buggered the fat woman.

There were also two men, their faces masked. Childe studied their bodies carefully, but he could not say that either was Igescu or Glam or the youth who had been playing billiards. One of the men had a build similar to Igescu's and another was a very big and muscular man. But he could not identify them as anyone he had seen at Igescu's.

Budler must have had a latent homosexual tendency which was developed, possibly under the influence of drugs, during the conditioning. One of the men blew him several times, and twice Budler buggered the big man. The third man appeared in one scene only, and this time it was in what Childe thought would be the grand finale. He braced himself for something terrible to happen to Budler, but aside from being exhausted, Budler seemed to suffer no ill effects. Budler and the three men and three women formed many configurations with, usually, Budler as the focus of the group.

The Commissioner, sitting by Childe, said at this point, 'This is quite an organization. Besides the six there, there must be two, at least, handling the cameras.'

The last scene (Childe knew it was the last because the Commissioner told him just as it flashed on) showed Budler screwing one of the well-built women dog-fashion. The cameras came in at every angle except that which would show the woman's face. There were a number of shots which must have been taken through a long flexible optical fibre device, because there were close-ups of a seemingly gargantuan penis driving in under a cavernous anus into an elephantine slit. The lubricating fluid flowed like spillage over a too-full dam.

And then the camera seemed to inch forward along the penis, now quiescent, and into the slit. Light blazed up, and the viewers seemed to be surrounded by thousands of tons of flesh. They were looking down at the penis, a whale that had crashed into an underseas cave. Then they were looking up at the ceiling of wet pale red flesh.

Suddenly, the light went out and they were back again, looking at Budler and the woman from the side. The two were on the bed, she face-down and her arms to one side and her buttocks raised by a pillow under her stomach. He was straddling her, one knee between the legs, and rocking back and forth.

Suddenly, so suddenly that Childe gasped and thought his heart would stop, the woman became a female wolf. Budler was still astride her and pumping slowly away when the transformation took place. (A trick of photography, of course. A trick involving drugs, surely, because Budler acted as if the woman had metamorphosed.) He stopped, raised his hands, and then sat up, his penis withdrawing and beginning to droop. He looked shocked.

Snarling, the wolf turned and slashed at his penis.

It happened so quickly that Childe did not understand immediately that the powerful jaws had taken the penis off close to the root.

Blood spurted out of the stump and over the wolf and the bed.

Screaming, Budler fell backward. The wolf bolted the penis down and then began biting at the man's testicles. Budler quit screaming. His skin turned blue-grey, and the camera left the wounds where the genitals had been and travelled up to show his dying face.

There was the tinny piano music again, Dvořák's *Humoresque*. The Dracula burst through the curtains with the same dramatic gesture of the cape thrown aside to reveal his face. The camera travelled down then and verified what Childe thought he had seen when the man entered but had not been certain about. The Dracula's penis, a very long and thin organ, was sticking out of the fly. The Dracula cackled and bounded forward and leaped upon the bed and grabbed the wolf by the hairs of its flanks and sank his penis into it from behind.

The wolf yowled, its mouth open, a piece of testicle falling out. Then, as the Dracula rammed it, driving her forward and inching along on his knees, the wolf began tearing at the flesh between the legs of Budler.

Fadeout. TO BE CONTINUED: in blazing white letters across the screen. End of film.

Childe became sick again. Afterward, he talked with the Commissioner, who was also pale and shaking. But he was not shaky in his refusal to take any action about Igescu. He explained (which Childe knew) that the evidence was too slight, in fact, it was nonexistent. The 'vampire' angle, the wolves on the estate, the (supposed) drugging of him by Igescu's secretary, the wolf hairs found in Budler's car, the wolf in the film, all these certainly would make investigation of Igescu legitimate. But Igescu was a very rich and powerful man with no known criminal records or any suspicions by the authorities of criminal connections. If the police were to do anything, and he did not see how they could, the Beverly Hills Police would have to handle the investigation.

The essence of his remarks was what Childe had expected. He would have to get more conclusive evidence, and he would have to do it without any help from the police.

Childe drove back through a darkening air. The weird white light was slowly turning green-grey. He stopped at a service station to fill his tank and also to replace the broken headlamp. The attendant, after stamping the form for his credit card, said, 'You may be my last customer. I'm taking off just as soon as I get the paperwork out of the way. Getting out of town, friend. This place has had it!'

91

'I may follow you,' Childe said. 'But I got some unfinished business to attend to first.'

'Yeah? This town's gonna be a ghost town; it's already on the way.'

Childe drove into Beverly Hills to shop. He had a difficult time finding a parking space. If it was going to be a ghost town, it did not seem that it would be so soon. Perhaps most of the people were getting supplies for the second exodus or were stocking up before the stores were again closed. Whatever the reason, it was two and a half hours before he got all he wanted, and it took a half-hour to drive the mile and a half to his apartment. The streets were again jammed with cars. Which, of course, only speeded up the poisoning of air.

Childe had intended to drive out to Igescu's at once, but he knew that he might as well wait until the traffic thinned out. He spent an hour reviewing what he meant to do and then tried to call Sybil, but the lines were busy again. He walked to her apartment. He was goggled and snouted with a gas mask he had purchased at a store which had just got a shipment in. So many others were similarly masked, the street looked like a scene on Mars.

Sybil was not home. Her car was still in the garage. The note he had left in her apartment was in the exact position in which he had placed it. He tried to get a long-distance call to her mother put through but had enough trouble getting the operator, who told him he would have to wait for a long time. She had been ordered to put through only emergency calls. He told her it *was* an emergency, his wife had disappeared and he wanted to find out if she had gone to San Francisco. The operator said that he would still have to wait, no telling how long. Should she call him back at that number when his turn came?

He said no and thank you and hung up. He walked back to his apartment and re-checked the automatic recorder with the same negative results. For a while he watched the news, most of which was a repetition or very slight updating of accounts of the smog and the emigration. It was too depressing, and he could not get interested in the only non-news programme, Shirley Temple in *Little Miss Marker*. He tried to read, but his mind kept jumping back and forth from Budler to his wife.

It was maddening not to be able to act. He almost decided to buck the traffic, because he might as well be doing something and, moreover, once off the main roads, he might be able to travel speedily. He looked out at the street, packed with cars going one way, horns blaring, drivers cursing out their windows or sitting stoic, tight-lipped, hands gripping the wheels. He would not be able to get his car out of the driveway.

At seven, the traffic suddenly became normal, as if a plug had been pulled some place and the extra vehicles gulped down it. He went into the basement, drove the car out, and got into the street without any trouble. A few cars drove down the wrong side, but these quickly pulled over into the right lane. He got to Igescu's before dusk; he had had to stop to change a flat tyre. The roads were littered with many objects, and one of these, a nail, had driven into his left rear tyre. Also, he was stopped by the police. They were looking for a service station robber driving a car of his make and colour. He satisfied them that he was not a criminal, not the one they were looking for, anyway, and continued on. The fact that they could concern themselves with a mere holdup at this time showed that the traffic had eased up considerably, in this area, at least.

At the end of the road outside Igescu's, he turned the car around and backed it into the bushes. He got out and, after removing the gas mask, raised the boot and took out the bundle he had prepared. It took him some time to carry the cumbersome load through the thick woods and up the hill to the wall. Here he unfolded the aluminium ladder, locked the joints, and, with the pack on his back, climbed up until his head was above the wire. He did not intend to find out if the wire was electrified. To do so might set off an alarm. He pulled up the long rubberized flexible tunnel, a child's plaything, by the rope tied around its end.

He hoisted it until half its length was over the wire and then began the unavoidably clumsy and slow manoeuvre of crawling, not into it but over it. His weight pressed it down so that he had a double thickness between him and the sharp points of the wire. He was able to turn, straddling the wire, and pull the ladder slowly up after him with the rope, which he had taken from the tunnel and tied to the ladder. He was very careful not to touch the wire with the ladder.

He lifted it up and turned it and deposited its end upon the ground on the inside of the wall. Once his feet were on the rungs, he lifted up the tunnel and dropped it on the ground and then climbed down. He repeated this procedure at the inner wall up to the point where he reached the top of the wall. Instead of climbing on over, he took two large steaks from his backpack and threw them as far as he could. Both landed upon leaves near the foot of a large oak. Then he pulled the tunnel back and retreated down the ladder. He sat with his back against the wall and waited. If he did not succeed with this step within two hours, he would go on in, anyway.

The darkness settled, but it did not seem to get any cooler. There was no air moving, no sound of bird or insect. The moon rose. A few minutes later, a howling jerked him to his feet. His scalp moved as if rubbed by a cold hand. The howling, distant at first, came closer. Soon there was a snuffling and then a growling and gobbling. Childe waited and checked his Smith & Wesson Terrier .32 revolver again. After five minutes by his wristwatch, he climbed over the wall, pulling the tunnel and ladder after him as he had done at the first wall. He laid them on the ground behind a tree in case anybody should be patrolling the wall. Gun in hand, he set out to look for the wolves. The bones of the steaks had been cracked and partially swallowed; the rest was gone.

He did not find the wolves. Or he was not sure that what he did find were the wolves.

He stepped into a clearing and then sucked in his breath.

Two bodies lay in the moonlight. They were unconscious, which state he had expected from the eating of drugged meat. But these were not the hairy, four-legged, long-muzzled bodies he had thought to see. These were the nude bodies of the young couple who had played billiards in the Igescu house. Vasili Chornkin and Mrs Krautschner slept on the grass under the moon. The boy was on his face, his legs under him and his hands by his face. The girl was on her side, her legs drawn up and her arms folded beside her head. She had a beautiful body. It reminded him of one of the girls he had seen in the films and especially of the girl Budler had been fucking dog style.

He had to sit down for a while. He felt shaky. He did not think that this was possible or impossible. It just *was*, and the *was* threatened him. It threatened his belief in the order of the universe, which meant that it threatened him.

After a while he was able to act. He used tape from his backpack to secure their hands behind them and their ankles together. Then he taped their mouths tightly and placed them on their sides, facing each other and as close together as possible and taped them together around the necks and the ankles. He was sweating by the time he had finished. He left them in the glade and hoped that they would be very happy together. (That he could think this showed him that he was recovering swiftly.) They should be happy if they knew that he had

94

planned to cut the throats of the wolves.

He headed towards where the house should be and within five minutes saw its bulk on top of the hill and some rectangles of light. Approaching it on the left, he stopped suddenly and almost fired his revolver, he was so upset by the abrupt appearance of the figure. It flitted from shadow into moonlight and back into shadow and was gone. It looked as if it were a woman wearing an ankle-length dress with a bare back.

For the third time that night, he felt a chill. It must have been Dolores. Or a woman playing the ghost. And why should a fraud be out here when there was no need to play the ghost? They did not know that he was here. At least, he hoped not.

It was possible that the baron wanted to shock another guest tonight and so was using this woman.

The driveway had five cars besides the Rolls-Royce Silver Cloud. There were two Cadillacs, a Lincoln, a Cord, and a 1929 Duesenberg. Neither wing showed a light, but the central part was well-lit.

Childe looked for Glam, did not see him, and went around the side. There was a vine-covered trellis which afforded easy access to the second storey balcony. The window was closed but not locked. The room was dark and hot and musty. He groped along the wall until he found a door and slowly swung it out. It opened on a closet in which hung dark musty clothes. He closed the door and felt along it until he discovered another door. This led to a hallway which was dimly lit by moonlight through a window. He used his pencil-thin flashlight now and then to guide himself. He passed by a stairway leading to the storey below and the storey above and pushed open a door to another hallway. This had no illumination at all; he fingered his way to the other end with his flashlight.

Sometimes he stopped to put his ear against a doorway. He had thought he had heard the murmurs of voices behind them. Intent listening convinced him that nobody was there, that his imagination was tricking him.

At the end of this hallway, twice as long as the first, he found a locked door. A series of keys left the lock unturned. He used his pick and, after several minutes work, during which the sweat ran down his eyes and his ribs and he had to stop several times because he thought he heard footsteps and, once, a breathing, he solved the puzzle of the tumblers.

The door opened to a shaft of light and a puff of cold air.

As he stepped through into the hallway, he caught a flash of something his left at the far end. It had moved too swiftly for him to identify it, but he thought that it was the tail end of Dolores' skirt. He ran down the hallway as quietly as he could with his sneakers on the marble tile floor (this was done in much-marbled and ornate-woodworked Victorian style even if it was in the Spanish part). At the corner, he halted and stuck his head around.

The woman at the extreme end was facing him. By the light of a floor lamp near her, he could see that she was tall and black-haired and beautiful – the woman in the portrait above the mantel in the drawing room.

She beckoned to him and turned and disappeared around the corner.

He felt a little disoriented, not so much as if he were being disconnected from a part of himself inside himself but as if the walls around him were being subtly warped.

Just as he rounded the corner, he saw her skirt going into a doorway. This led to a room halfway down the hall. The only light was that from the lamp on a stand in the hallway. He groped around until he felt the light switch. The response was the illumination of a small lamp at the other end on a stand by a huge bed with a canopy. He did not know much about furniture, but it looked like a bed from one of the Louis series, Louis Quatorze, perhaps. The rest of the expensive-looking furniture seemed to go with the bed. A large crystal chandelier hung from the centre of the ceiling.

The wall was white panelling, and one of the panels was just swinging shut.

Childe thought it was swinging shut. He had blinked, and then the wall seemed solid.

There was no other way for the woman to have gone.

Do ghosts have to open doors, or panels, to go from one room to another?

Perhaps they did, if they existed. However, he had seen nothing to indicate that Dolores – or whoever the woman was – must be a ghost.

If she were a hoax set up by Baron Igescu for the benefit of others, and particularly for Childe, she was leading him on for a reason that he could only believe was sinister. The panel led to a passage between the walls, and Igescu must want him to go through the panel.

The newspaper article had said that the original house had

contained between-walls passages and underground passages and several secret tunnels which led to exits in the woods. Don del Osorojo had built these because he feared attacks from bandits, wild Indians, revolting peasants, and, possibly, government troops. The Don, it seemed, was having trouble with tax-collectors; the government claimed that he was hiding gold and silver.

When the first Baron Igescu, the present owner's uncle, had added the wings, he had also built secret passageways which connected to those in the central house. Not so secret, actually, since the workers had talked about them, but no drawings or blueprints of the house's construction existed, as far as anybody knew. And most of the workers would now be dead or so old they could not remember the layout, even if any of them could be found.

The panel had been opened long enough for him to know that it was an entrance. Perhaps the baron wanted him to know it; perhaps Dolores, the ghost. In any event, he meant to go through it.

Finding the actuator of the entrance was another matter. He pressed the wood around the panel, tried to move strips around it, knocked at various places on the panel (it sounded hollow), and examined the wood closely for holes. He found nothing out-of-the-way.

Straightening up, he half-turned in an angry movement and then turned back again, as if he would catch something – or somebody – doing something behind his back. There was nothing behind him that had not been there before. But he did glimpse himself in the huge floor-to-ceiling mirror that constituted half of the wall across the room.

13

The mirror certainly was not reflecting as a mirror should. Nor was it reflecting grossly or exaggeratedly, like a funny-house mirror. The distortions – if they could be called distortions – were subtle. And as evasive as drops of mercury.

There were slight shiftings of everything reflected, of the wall behind him, the painting on the wall to one side of him, the canopied bed, and himself. It was as if he were looking at an underwater room through a window, with himself deep in the water and the mirror a window, or porthole, to a room in a subaquatic palace. The objects in the room, and he seemed to be as much an object as the bed or a chair, swayed a little. As if currents of cold water succeeded by warmer water compressed or expanded the water and so changed the intensity and the refraction of lighting.

There was more to the shifting than that, however. At one place, the room and everything in it, including himself, seemed almost – not quite – normal. As they should be or as it seemed that they should be. Seemed, he thought, because it struck him that things as they are were not necessarily things as they should be, that custom had made strangeness, or outrageousness (a peculiar word, what made him think of that?), comfortable.

Then the 'normality' disappeared as the objects twisted or swayed, he was not sure which they did, and the room, and he, became 'evil'.

He did not look 'weak' nor 'petty' nor 'sneaky' nor 'selfish' nor 'indifferent' all of which he felt himself to be at various times. He looked 'evil'. Malignant, destroying, utterly loveless.

He walked slowly towards the mirror. His image, wavering, advanced. It smiled, and he suddenly realized that he was smiling. That smile was not utterly loveless; it was a smile of pure love. Love of hatred of and the corruption of all living things.

He could almost smell the stink of hate and of death.

Then he thought that the smile was not of love but of greed, unless greed was a form of love. It could be.

The meanings of words were as shifting and elusive as the images in the mirror.

He became sick; something was gnawing at his nerves in the pit of his stomach.

It was a form of sea-sickness, he thought. See-sickness, rather.

He turned away from the mirror, feeling as he did so a chill pass over his scalp and a vulnerability – a hollowness – between his shoulders, as if the man in the mirror would stick him in the back with a knife if he exposed his back to him.

He hated the mirror and the room it mirrored. He had to get out of it. If he could not get the panel open in a few seconds, he would have to leave by the door.

There was no use in repeating his first efforts. The key to the panel was not in its immediate neighbourhood, so he would have to look elsewhere. Perhaps its actuator, a button, a stud, something, could be behind the large oil painting. This was of a man who looked much like the baron and was probably his uncle. Childe lifted it up and off its hooks and placed it upright on the floor, leaning against the wall. The space behind where it had been was smooth. No actuator mechanism here.

He replaced the painting. It seemed twice as heavy when he lifted it up as it had when he had taken it down. This room was draining him of his strength.

He turned away from the painting and stopped. The panel had swung inward into the darkness behind the wall.

Childe, keeping an eye on the panel, placed a hand on the lower corner of the portrait-frame and moved it slightly. The panel, however, had already started to close. Evidently the actuating mechanism opened it briefly and then closed it automatically.

He waited until the panel shut and again moved the frame sideways. Nothing happened. But when he lifted the painting slightly, the panel again swung open.

Childe did not hesitate. He ran to the panel, stepped through cautiously, making sure that there was firm footing in the darkness, and then got to one side to permit the panel to swing shut. He was in unrelieved black; the air was dead and odorous of decaying wood, plaster falling apart, and a trace of long-dead mice. There was also a teaser (was it there or not?) of perfume.

The flashlight showed a dusty corridor about four feet wide and seven high. It did not end against the wall of the hallway, as he had expected. A well of blackness turned out to be a stairway under the hall. At its bottom was a small platform and another stairway leading up, he presumed, to another passageway on the other side of the hall.

In the opposite direction, the passageway ran straight for about fifty feet and then disappeared around a corner. He walked slowly in that direction and examined the walls, ceiling, and floor carefully. When he had gone far enough to be past the baron's bedroom, he found a panel on hinges. It was too small and too far up the wall for passage. He unlocked its latch, turned his flashlight off, and swung it slowly out to avoid squeaking of hinges. They gave no sound. The panel hid a one-way mirror. He was looking into a bedroom. A titian-haired woman came through the door from the hall about seven seconds later. She walked past him, only five feet away, and disappeared into another doorway. She was wearing a print dress with large red flowers; her legs were bare and her feet were sandalled.

The woman was so beautiful that he had felt sick in his solar plexus for a moment, a feeling he had experienced three times, when seeing for the first time women so beautiful that he was agonized because he would never have them.

Childe thought that it would be better to continue his exploring, but he could not resist the feeling that he might see something significant if he stayed there. The woman had looked so determined, as if she had something important to do. He placed his ear against the glass and could hear, faintly, Richard Strauss' *Thus Spake Zarathustra.* It must be coming from the room into which she had gone.

The bedroom was in rather sombre taste for a beautiful young woman; the baron's room, if it had been the baron's room, would have been more appropriate for her. It was far cheerier, if you excepted the wall-mirror. The walls were of dark dull wooden panelling about six feet up from the floor; above them was a dull dark wallpaper with faint images: queer birds, twisted dragons, and the recurring figures of what could be a nude Adam and Eve and an apple tree. There were no snakes.

The carpet was thick and also dull and dark with images too faded to be identified. The bed was, like the baron's, canopied, but it was of a period he did not recognize, although this did not mean much, because he knew very little about furniture or furnishings. Its legs were wrought-iron in the form of dragons' claws, the bedspread and the canopy were a dark red. There was a mirror on the wall opposite. It was three-sided, like the mirrors used in the clothing departments of stores. It seemed to be nothing extraordinary; it reflected the window through which Childe was looking as another mirror above a large dull red-brown dresser.

There was a chandelier of cut quartz with dull yellow sockets for

100

candles. The light in the room, however, came from a number of table and floor lamps. The corners of the room were in shadow.

Childe waited for a while and sweated. It was hot in the corridor, and the various odours, of wood, plaster, and long-dead mice, became stronger instead of dying on a dulling nose. The teaser of perfume was entirely gone. Finally, just as he decided that he should be moving on – and why was he standing here in the first place – the woman came through the door. She was naked; her titian-red hair hung loosely around her shoulders and down her back. She held a long-necked bottle to her lips as she walked towards the dresser. She paused before it and continued to drink until only about two inches of the liquid was left. Then she put the bottle on the dresser and leaned forward to look into the mirror.

She had taken her make-up off. She peered into the mirror as if she were searching for defects. Childe stepped back, because it seemed impossible that she would not see him. Then he stepped forward again. If she knew that this was a one-way mirror, she did not care if another was on the other side. Or supposed that no hostile person would be there. Perhaps only the baron knew of this passageway.

She seemed to find her inspection of her face satisfactory, and she might have found it very pleasing, to judge from her smile. She straightened up and looked at her body and also seemed pleased at this. Childe felt uncomfortable, as if he were doing something perverted by spying on her, but he also began to get excited.

She wriggled a little, swayed her hips from side to side, and ran her hands up and down her ribs and hips and then cupped them over her breasts and rubbed the nipples with the ends of her thumbs. The nipples swelled. Childe's penis swelled, also.

Keeping her left hand busy with her breast, she put her right hand on her pubes, and opened the top of the slit with one finger and began to rub her clitoris. She worked swiftly at it, rubbing vigorously, and suddenly she threw her head back, her mouth open, ecstasy on her face.

Childe felt both excited and repulsed. Part of the repulsion was because he was no voyeur; he felt that it was indecent to watch anyone under these circumstances. It was true that he did not have to stay, but he was here to investigate kidnapping and murder, and this certainly looked worth investigating.

She continued to rub her clitoris and the hairy lips. And then – here Childe was startled and shaken but also knew that he had

101

somehow expected it – a tiny thing, like a slender white tongue, spurted from the slit.

It was not a tongue. It was more like a snake or an eel.

It was as small in diameter as a garter snake but much longer. How long it was he could not determine yet, because its body kept sliding out and out. It kept coming, and its skin was smooth and hairless, as smooth as the woman's belly and as white, and the skin glistened with the fluid from her cunt.

It shot out in a downward arc, like a half-erect penis, and then it turned and flopped over against her belly and began to zigzag upwards. It continued to slide out from the slit as if yards of it were still coiled inside her womb, and it continued to ooze up until its snaky length was coiled once around her left breast.

Childe could see the details of the thing's head, which was the size of a golf ball. It turned twice to look directly at him. Into the mirror, rather.

Its head was bald except for a fringe of oil-plastered black hair around the tiny ears. It had two thin but wet black eyebrows and a wet black Mephistophelean moustache and beard. The nose was relatively large and meat cleaver shaped. The eyes were dark, but they were so small and set so far back that they would have seemed dark to Childe even if they had been palest blue. The mouth was as much a slit as the vagina from which the creature had issued, but it briefly opened its mouth, and Childe could see two rows of little yellow teeth and a pink-red tongue.

The face was tiny, but there was nothing feeble about its malignancy.

The woman's lips moved. Childe could not hear her, but he thought that she was crooning.

The snake body resumed its climbing while more of its body slid out of the pink fissure and the dark-red bush. It rounded her breast and went up her shoulder and around her neck and came around the right side and extended a loop outwards and then in so that the Lilliputian head faced her. The woman turned a little then, thus permitting Childe a quarter-view of her profile.

Her hands moved along the ophidian shaft as if she were feeling an unnaturally long penis – hers. Her slim fingers – beautiful fingers – traced the length and then, while one hand curled gently around the back of the head to support the body, the other slid back and forth from a few inches behind the head on down to the slit, as if she were masturbating the snake-penis.

The thing quivered. Then the head moved forward, and its minute lips touched her lower lip. It bit down, or seemed to, because she jerked her head back a little as if stung. Her head moved forward again, however, and her mouth was wide open. The head was engulfed in her mouth; she began to suck.

Childe had been too shocked to do anything but react emotionally. Now he began to think. He wondered how the thing could breathe with its head in her mouth. Then it occurred to him that it would be even more difficult for it to breathe when it was coiled in her womb or whatever recess of her body it lived in. So, though it had a nose, it perhaps did not need it. Its oxygen could be supplied by the woman's circulatory system, which surely must be connected through some umbilical device to the other end of the thing.

That head. It had belonged at one time to a full-grown man. Childe, with no rational reason, knew this. The head had belonged to the body of an adult male. Now, through some unbelievable science, the head had been reduced to the size of a golf ball, and it had been attached to this uterine snake, or the original human body had been altered, or . . .

He shook his head. How could this be? Had he been drugged? That mirror and now this.

The body bent, and the head withdrew from the woman's mouth. It swayed back and forth like a cobra to a flute, while the woman put her hands to her mouth and then removed a set of false teeth. Her lips fell in; she was an old woman – from the neck up. But the thing thrust forward before she had put the teeth on the dresser, and the tiny head and part of the body disappeared into the toothless cavity. The body bent and unbent, slid back and forth between her lips.

At first, the movements were slow. Then her body trembled, and her skin became paler, except around the mouth and the pubes, where the intense darkening spoke of the concentration of blood. She shook; her great eyes fluttered open; she stared as if she were half-stunned. The thrustings of the body became swifter, and more of the body appeared and disappeared. She staggered backwards until she fell back upon the bed with her legs hanging over the edge and one foot resting on the floor, the other lifted up.

For perhaps ninety seconds, she jerked. Then, she was quiet. The snaky body lifted; the head came out of the lips and turned with the turning of the upper quarter of body. A thick whitish fluid was dribbling out of the open mouth.

The shaft rose up and up until all but the last six inches were lifted from the woman's body. It teetered like a sunflower in a flood and then collapsed. The tiny mouth chewed on a nipple for a while. The woman's hands moved like sleeping birds half-roused by a noise, then they became quiet again.

The mouth quit chewing. The body began a slow zigzag retreat into the dark-red bush and the fissure, trailing the head behind it. Presently, the body was gone and the head was swallowed up, bulging open the labia as it sank out of sight.

Childe thought, Werewolf? Vampire? Lamia? Vodyanoi? What?

He had never read of anything like this woman and the thing in her womb. Where did they fit in with the theories of Le Garrault as expounded by Igescu?

The woman rose from the bed and walked to the dresser. Looking into the mirror, she fitted the false teeth into her mouth and once more was the most beautiful woman in the world.

But she was also the most horrifying woman he had ever seen. He was shaking as much as she had been in her orgasm, and he was sick.

At that moment, the door that opened on to the hallway moved inward.

Childe felt as cold as if he had been dipped into an opening in polar ice.

The pale-skinned, scarlet-lipped, black-haired head of Dolores del Osorojo had appeared around the doorway.

The woman, who must have seen Dolores in the mirror, greyed. Her mouth dropped open; saliva and the spermy fluid dribbled out. Her eyes became huge. Her hands flew up – like birds again – to cover her breasts. Then she screamed so loudly that Childe could hear her, and she whirled and ran towards the door. She had snatched up the bottle by the neck so swiftly that Childe was not aware of it until she was halfway across the room. She was terrified. No doubt about that. But she was also courageous. She was attacking the cause of her terror.

Dolores smiled, and a white arm came around the door and pointed at the woman.

The woman stopped, the bottle raised above her head, and she quivered.

Then Childe saw that Dolores was not pointing at the woman. She was pointing past her. At him.

At the mirror behind which he stood rather. The woman whirled and looked at it and then, bewildered, looked around. Again, she whirled, and this time she shouted something in an unidentifiable language at the woman. The woman smiled once more, withdrew her arm, and then her head. The door closed.

Shaking, the woman walked slowly to the door, slowly opened it, and slowly looked through the doorway into the hall. If she saw anything, she did not care to pursue it, because she closed the door. She emptied the bottle then and returned to the dresser, where she pulled up a chair and sat down on it and then put her head on her arms on the table. After a while, the pinkish glow returned to her skin. She sat up again. Her eyes were bright with tears and her face seemed to have got about ten years older. She leaned close to the mirror to look at it, grimaced, got up, and went through the other door, which Childe presumed led to a bathroom or to a room which led to a bathroom.

Her reaction to Dolores certainly was not the baron's, who had seemed blasé, or even her reaction when she had seen Dolores in the living room. But here, where she was alone, the sight of the supposed ghost had terrified her.

If Dolores were a hoax, one of which the woman would surely be aware, why should she react so?

Childe had a more-than-uneasy feeling that Dolores del Osorojo was not a woman hired to play ghost.

It was, however, possible that the woman was terrified for other reasons.

He had no time to find out what. He used the flashlight in quick stabs to determine if there was an entrance to her room, but he could find none. He went on then and came across another panel which opened to another one-way mirror. This showed him a small living room done in Spanish colonial style. Except for the telephone on a table, it could have been a room in the house shortly after it was built. There was nobody in it.

The corridor turned past the room. Along the wall here was a hinged panel large enough to give entrance to the other side. There was also a peephole behind a small sliding panel. He put his eye to it but could see only a darkened room. At the periphery of his vision was a lightening of the darkness, as if light were leaking through a barely opened door or a keyhole. A voice was coming from somewhere far off. It was in a strange language, and it seemed to be carrying on a monologue or a telephone conversation.

Beyond this room the corridor became two, the legs of a Y. He went down each for a short distance and found that two entrance panels existed on opposite walls of one leg and an entrance panel and peephole on opposite walls of the other. If, at another time, he could locate a triangular-shaped room, he would know where these passageways were.

He looked through the peephole but could see nothing. He went back up the passageway and up the other leg to the panel and opened this. His hand, thrust through the opening, felt a heavy cloth. He slid through carefully so that he would not push the cloth. It could be a drapery heavy enough to keep light on the other side from shining through. If anybody were in that room, he must not see the drapery move.

Squatting, his shoulder to the wall and squeezing his shoulders so that he would not disturb the cloth, he duck-walked until he had come to the juncture of two walls. Here the edges of the draperies met. He turned and pulled the edges apart and looked through with one eye.

The room was dark. He rose and stepped through and turned his flashlight on. The beam swept across a movie camera on a dolly and then stopped on a Y-shaped table.

He was in the room, or one much like it, in which Colben and Budler had spent their – presumably – last few hours.

There was a bed in one corner, a number of movie cameras, some devices the use of which he did not know, and a large ashtray of some dark-green material. In the centre of its roughly circular dish stood a long thin statue. It looked like a nude man in the process of turning into a wolf, or vice versa. The body up to the chest was human; from there on it was hairy and the arms had become legs and the face had wolf-like ears and was caught in metamorphosis. There were about thirty cigarette stubs in the dish. Some had lipstick marks. One had a streak of dried blood, or it looked like dried blood, around the filter.

Childe turned on the lights and with the tiny Japanese camera took twenty shots. He had what he needed now, and he should get out. But he did not know whether or not Sybil was in this house.

And there might be other, even more impressive, evidence to get the police here.

He turned off the lights and crawled out of the panel into the passageway. He had a choice of routes then and decided to take the right leg of the Y. This led to another hall – the horizontal bar of a T. He turned right again and came to a stairway. The treads were of a glassy substance; it would have been easy to slip on them if he had not been wearing sneakers. He walked down six steps, and then his feet slid out from under him and he fell heavily on his back.

He struck a smooth slab and shot downward as if on a chutey-chute, which, in a sense, he was on. He put out his hands against the walls to brake himself but the walls, which had not seemed vitreous, were. The flashlight showed him a trapdoor opening at the bottom of the steps – these had straightened out to fall against each other and form a smooth surface – and then he slid through the dark opening. He struck heavily but was unhurt. The trapdoor closed above him. The flashlight showed him the padded ceiling, walls, and floor of a room seven feet high, six broad, ten deep. There were no apparent doors or windows.

He smelled nothing nor heard anything, but gas must have been let into the room. He fell asleep before he knew what was happening.

14

He did not know how long he had been there. When he awoke, his flashlight, his wristwatch, his revolver, and his camera were missing. His head ached, and his mouth was as dry as if he were waking up after a three-day drunk. The gas must have had a very relaxing effect, because he had wet his shorts and pants. Or else he had wet them when the steps had dropped out from under him and he had begun his slide. He had needed to piss just before the trap caught him.

Five lights came on. Four were from floor-lamps set in the corners, and one was from an iron wall-lamp shaped like a torch and set at forty-five degrees to the wall.

He was not in the padded chamber. He was lying on a huge four-poster bed with scarlet sheets and bedspread and a scarlet black-edged canopy. The room was not one he had seen before. It was large; its black walls were hung with scarlet yellow-trimmed drapes and two sets of crossed rapiers. The floor was dark-glossy brown hardwood with a few crimson starfish-shaped thick-fibred rugs. There were some slender wrought-iron chairs with high skeletal backs and crimson cushions on the seats and a tall dresser of dense-grained brown wood.

It was while looking around that he thought of the dread of iron and of the cross that vampires were supposed to have. There were iron objects all over the house, and, while he had seen no crucifixes, he had seen plenty of objects, such as these crossed rapiers, which made cruciforms. If Igescu was a vampire (Childe felt ridiculous even thinking this), he certainly did not object to contact with iron or sight of the cross.

Perhaps (just perhaps), these creatures had acquired an immunity from these once-abhorred things during thousands of years. If they *had* ever dreaded iron and the cross, that is. What about the years before iron was used by man? Or the cross was used by man? What guards and wards did man have then against these creatures?

Shakily, Childe got out of the bed and stood up. He had no time to search for a secret wall-exit, which he thought could exist here and which he might find before his captors returned. But the door at the far end swung open, and Glam entered, and the big room seemed much smaller. He stopped very close to Childe and looked down at him. For the first time, Childe saw that his eyes were light russet. The face was heavy and massive as a boulder, but those eyes seemed to glow as if they were rocks which had been subjected to radioactivity. Hairs hung from the cavernous nostrils like stalactites. His breath stank as if he had been eating rotten octopus.

'The baron says you should come to dinner,' he rumbled.

'In these clothes?'

Glam looked down at the wet patch on the front of Childe's pants. When he looked up, he smiled briefly, like a jack-o'lantern just before the candle died.

'The baron says you can dress if you want to. There's clothes your size or near enough in the closet.'

The closet was almost big enough to be a small room. His eyebrows rose when he saw the variety of male and female clothing. Who were the owners and where were they? Were they dead? Did some of the clothes bear labels with the names of Colben and Budler, or had they borne the labels, since the baron would not be stupid enough, surely, to leave such identification on.

Perhaps he *was* stupid. Otherwise, why the sending of the films to the Los Angeles Police Department?

But he did not really believe this about the baron.

Childe, after washing his hands and face and genitals and thighs in the most luxurious bathroom he had ever been in, and after dressing in a tuxedo, followed Glam down several hallways and then downstairs. He did not recognize any of the corridors nor the dining room. He had expected to be in the dining room he had seen yesterday, but this was another. The house was truly enormous.

The motif of this room was, in some respects, Early Grandiose Victorian-Italian, or so it seemed to him. The walls were grey black-streaked marble. A huge red marble fireplace and mantel were at one end, and above the mantel was a painting of a fierce old white-haired man with long moustachioes. He wore a wine-red coat with wide lapels and a white shirt with thick ruffles around the neck.

The floor was of black marble with small mosaics at each of the eight corners. The furniture was massive and of a black dense-grained wood. A white damascene cloth covered the main table; it was set with massive silver dishes and goblets and tableware and tall thick silver candle-holders which supported thick red candles. There were at least fifty candles, all lit. A large cut-quartz chandelier held a number of red candles, also, but these were unlit.

Glam stopped to indicate a chair. Childe advanced slowly to it. The baron, at the head of the table, rose to greet him. His smile was broad but fleeting. He said, 'Welcome, Mr Childe, despite the circumstances. Please sit down there. Next to Mrs Grasatchow.'

There were four men and six women at the table.

The baron.

Magda Holyani.

Mrs Grasatchow, who was almost the fattest woman he had ever seen.

The baron's great-grandmother, who had to be at least a hundred.

Vivienne Mabcrough, the titian-haired woman with the man-headed snake-thing in her womb.

O'Riley O'Faithair, a handsome black-haired man of about thirty-five who spoke a charming Irish brogue. And now and then a few sentences in an unknown language to the baron and the Mabcrough woman.

Mr Bending Grass, who had a very broad and high-cheekboned face with a huge aquiline nose and huge, slightly slanted, very dark eyes. He could have been Sitting Bull's twin, but something he said to Mrs Grasatchow indicated that he was Crow. He spoke of the mountain man, John Johnston, 'Liver Eating Johnston', as if he had been a contemporary.

Fred Pao, a tall slender Chinese with features that could have been carved out of teak and a Fu Manchu moustache and goatee.

Panchita Pocyotl, a short petite and beautiful Mexican Indian.

Rebecca Ngima, a handsome lithe black African dressed in a long white native costume.

They were all expensively and tastefully dressed and, though their speech was not free of foreign pronunciation, their English was fluent, 'correct', and rich with literary, philosophical, historical, and musical allusions. There were also references to events and persons and places that puzzled Childe, who was well-read. They seemed to have been everywhere and, here he felt cold threading the needle of his nerves, to have lived in times long dead.

Was this for his benefit? An addition to the hoax?

What hoax?

It was then that he got another shock, because the baron addressed him again as Mr Childe. With a start, he remembered the

110

first time. He had been too dull to have realized then what that meant.

'How did you learn my name?' he said. 'I carried no identification with me.'

The baron smiled and said, 'You don't really expect me to tell you?'

Childe shrugged and began eating. There were many different dishes on the sideboard; he had been given a wide choice but had decided on New York-cut steak and baked potato. Mrs Grasatchow, who sat on his left, had a platter with an entire bonita fish and a huge bowl of salad. She drank before, during, and after the meal from a gallon decanter of bourbon. The decanter was full when she sat down and empty when the dishes were cleared off the table.

Glam and two short, dark, and shapely women in maids' uniforms served. The women did not act like servants, however, they frequently talked with the guests and the host and several times made remarks in the foreign tongue that caused the others to laugh. Glam spoke only when his duties required. He glanced at Magda far more than his duties required.

The baroness, seated at the opposite end from her great-grandson, bent like a living question mark, or vulture, over her soup. This was the only food she was served, and she allowed it to get cold before she finally finished it. She said very little and only looked up twice, once to stare a long time at Childe. She looked as if she had only recently been brought out of an Egyptian pyramid and as if she would just as soon go back into the crypt. Her dinner gown, high-necked, ruffle-bosomed, diamond-sequined, red velvet, looked as if she had purchased it in 1890.

Mrs Grasatchow, although as fat as two sows put together, had a remarkably white, flawless, and creamy skin and enormous purplish eyes. When she had been younger and thinner, she must have been a beautiful woman. She talked now as if she thought she was still beautiful, perhaps the most beautiful and desirable woman in the world. She talked loudly and uninhibitedly about the men who had died – some of them literally – for her love. Halfway through the dinner, and two-thirds through the gallon of whisky, her speech began to get slurred. Childe was awed. She had drunk enough to kill him, or most men, and she only had a little trouble with her speech.

She had drunk far more than the Chinese, Pao, who had downed

111

much wine during the evening, but not much relative to her. Yet nobody reprimanded her, but Igescu seemed concerned about Pao. He was speaking to him in a corner, and though Childe could not hear them, he saw Igescu's hand come down on Pao's wrist, and Igescu shook his head and then jerked the thumb of his other hand at Childe.

Suddenly, Pao began to shake, and he ran out of the room. He was in a hurry to get out, but Childe did not think that he was about to vomit. He did not have the pale skin and desperate expression of one whose guts are ready to launch their contents.

The dishes were cleared and cigars and brandy and wine were served. (My God! was Mrs Grasatchow really going to smoke that ten-dollar cigar and pour down a huge snifter of brandy on top of that whisky?)

The baron spoke to Childe:

'You realize, of course, that I could easily have had you killed for trespassing, for entering, for voyeurism, et cetera, but mostly for entering? Now, perhaps, you would like to tell me what you are up to?'

Childe hesitated. The baron knew his name and must, therefore, know that he was a private investigator. And that he had been a partner of Colben. He must realize that, somehow, Childe had tracked him down, and he must be curious about what had led Childe here. He might be wondering if Childe had told anybody that he was coming out here.

Childe decided to be frank. He also decided that he would tell the baron that the LAPD knew he was here and that if they did not hear from him at a certain time, they would come out here to find out why.

Igescu listened with a smile that seemed amused. He said, 'Of course! And what would they find if they did come out here, which they are not likely to do?'

Perhaps they would find something Igescu did not suspect. They might find two naked people tied to each other. Igescu might have a difficult time explaining them, but they would not be a dangerous liability. Just puzzling to the police and inconvenient to Igescu.

At that moment Vasili Chornkin and Mrs Krautschner, fully clothed, entered. They stopped for a moment, stared at Childe, and then walked on in. The blonde stopped by Igescu to whisper in his ear; the man sat down and ordered something to eat. Igescu looked at Childe, frowned, and then smiled. He said something to Mrs Krautschner. She laughed and sat down by Chornkin.

Childe felt even more trapped. He could do nothing except, perhaps, make a break for it, but he doubted that he would get far. There was nothing for him to do except drift with the current of Igescu's wishes and hope that he would get a chance to escape.

The baron, looking over the brandy snifter just below his nose, said, 'Did you get a chance to read Le Garrault, Mr Childe?'

'No, I didn't. But I understand the UCLA library is closed because of the smog.'

The baron stood up. 'Let's go into the library and talk where it's quieter.'

Mrs Grasatchow heaved up from the chair, blowing like an alcoholic whale. She put an arm around Childe's shoulder; the flesh drooped like tangles of jungle vines. 'I'll go with you, baby, you don't want to go without me.'

'You can stay here for the time being,' Igescu said.

Mrs Grasatchow glared at the baron, but she dropped her arm from Childe and sat down.

The library was a large dark room with dark leather-covered walls and massive dark-wood built-in shelves and at least five thousand books, some of them looking centuries old. The baron sat down in an overstuffed leather-covered chair with a wooden back carved in the form of a bat-winged Satan. Childe sat down in a similar chair, the back of which was carved as a troll.

'Le Garrault . . .' the baron said.

'What's going on here?' Childe said. 'Why the party?'

'You aren't interested in Le Garrault?'

'Sure, I'm interested. But I think there are things of much more interest just now. For instance, my survival.'

'That is up to you, of course. One's survival is always up to one's self. Other people only play the part that you permit. But then, that's another theory. For the present, let's pretend that you are my guest and may leave at any time you wish – which can be the true situation. For all you know. Believe me, I am not telling you about Le Garrault just to pass the time. Am I?'

The baron continued to smile. Childe thought about Sybil and got angry. But he knew that it would do no good to ask the baron about her. If the baron had her, he would admit it only if it served some purpose of his.

'The old Belgian scholar knew more about the occult and the supernatural and the so-called *weird* than any other man who ever lived. I don't mean that he knew more than *anybody* else. I mean that he knew more than any other *man*.'

The baron paused to draw in cigar smoke. Childe felt himself getting tense, although he was making an effort to relax.

'Old Le Garrault found records which other scholars did not find or else saw in these records what other scholars missed. Or possibly he may have talked to some of the – what should I call them? Unmen? – some of the unmen, the pseudo-men, and got his facts, which we shall call theory, directly from them.

'In any event, Le Garrault speculated that the so-called vampires, werewolves, poltergeists, ghosts, and so on, might be living creatures from a parallel universe. You know what a parallel universe is?'

'It's a concept originated by some science-fiction author, I believe,' Childe said. 'I think that the theory is that a number, perhaps an infinite number, of universes may occupy the same space. They can do this because they are all *polarized* or *at right angles* to each other. Those terms are actually meaningless, but they do signify that some physical mechanism enables more than one cosmos to fill the same quote *space* unquote. The concept of parallel universes was used and is being used by science-fiction writers to depict worlds just like ours, or only slightly differing, or wildly different. Like a universe where the South won the Civil War. That idea has been used at least three times, that I know of.'

'Very good,' the baron said. 'Except that your examples are not quite correct. None of the three stories you are thinking about postulated a parallel universe. Churchill's and Kantor's were *what if* stories, and Moore's was a time travel story. But you have the right idea. However, Le Garrault was the first to publish the theory of parallel universes, although the publication was so restricted and so obscure that very few people knew about it. And Le Garrault did not postulate a series of universes which diverged only slightly at one end of the series, that is, the end nearest to Earth's cosmos, and diverged more the further away you got from the Earth's.

'No, he speculated that these other universes were nothing at all like Earth's, that they had different physical "laws", that many of them would be completely incomprehensible to Earthmen who might broach the "walls" between the universes.'

'Then he said that there might be "gates" or "breaks" in the "walls" and that occasionally a dweller of one universe might go into another?'

'He said more than that. He called his speculation a theory, but he believed that the theory was a fact. He believed that there were temporary breaks in the walls, accidental cracks, or openings which sometimes existed because of weaknesses or flaws.

'He said that creatures – sentient and non-sentient – sometimes entered our universe through these breaks. But they have forms so alien that the human brain has no forms to *explain* them. He said that it was not just a matter of humans *seeing* the aliens as such and such. It is a matter of the aliens actually being moulded into these forms because they cannot survive long in this universe unless they have forms that conform to the physical "laws" of this universe. The forms may not conform one hundred percent, but they are close enough. And, in fact, an alien may have more than one form, because that is the way the human sees him. Hence, the werewolf, who has a human form and wolf form, and the vampire, who has a human form and a bat form.'

This man is really putting me on, Childe thought. Or else he is so insane that he actually believes this. But what is he leading up to, that he is one of the aliens?

The baron said, 'Some of the extra-universals came here accidentally, were caught in the flaws, and were unable to get back. Others were exiles or criminals, sent by the people of their world to this Botany Bay – this Earth.'

'Fascinating speculation,' Childe said. 'But why do these take certain forms and not others?'

'Because, in their case, the myth, the legend, the superstition, call it what you will, gave birth to the reality. First, there were the beliefs and tales about the werebeast and the vampire and the ghost and the et cetera. These beliefs and tales existed long ago, long before history, long before civilization. In one form or another, these beliefs existed in the Old Stone Age.'

Childe shifted to relieve his discomfort. He felt cold again. He felt as if a shadow had slid over him. That shadow was of a great hulking half-brute figure, bulge-browed, ape-jawed. And behind it were other shadows of figures with long fangs and great claws and strange shapes.

The baron continued, 'There is, according to Le Garrault, a *psychic imprinting*. He did not use the word *imprinting*, but his description meant that. He said that the aliens are able to survive for a short while in their own form when they come to this universe. They are in a state of fluidity, of dying fluidity.'

'Fluidity?'

'Their forms are trying to change to conform to the physical laws of this universe. A universe which is as incomprehensible to them as theirs would be to an Earthman. The effort sets up stresses and strains which would inevitably tear them apart, kill them. Unless they encounter a human being. And, if they are lucky enough to be from a universe which enables them to receive – telepathically, I suppose, although that term is too restricted – enables them to receive the impressions of the human mind, then the alien is able to make the adaptation. He is enabled because he comprehends the form in which he can survive in this world. Do you follow me?'

'In a way. But not too well.'

'It's almost as difficult to explain this as it is for a mystic to explain his visions. You realize that my explanations no more fit the facts, the true processes, than the description of the atom as a sort of miniature solar system fitted the true processes.'

'I understand that, at least. You're using analogies.'

'Strained analogies. But the theory says that the alien, if he is lucky, encounters human beings who perceive him as something unnatural, which he is, in a sense, since he is not natural to the human universe. The humans do not absolutely reject him; it is the nature of humans to try to explain every phenomenon or, should I say, describe it, classify it, fit it into the order of natural things.

'And so the alien is given his form, and a certain part of his nature, by the humans. There is a process of *psychic imprinting*, you understand. And so, willynilly, the alien becomes what the human believes him to be. But the alien still retains some of his otherworld characteristics, or I should say powers or abilities, and these he can use under certain circumstances. He can use them because they are part of the structure of this universe, even though most humans, that is, the educated, that is, the reconditioned, deny that such powers, or even such beings, can exist in this universe.'

'You were enjoying your filet mignon and your salad,' Childe said. 'I thought vampires lived only on blood?'

'Who said I was a vampire?' the baron replied, smiling. 'Or who said that vampires live on blood only? Or, who, saying that, knew what he was talking about?'

'Ghosts,' Chidle said. 'How does this theory explain ghosts?'

'Le Garrault said that ghosts are the results of imperfect *psychic imprinting*. In their case, they assume, partially assume, the form of the human being first encountered or, sometimes, they result from the belief of a human being that they are the ghost of a departed. Thus, a man who believes in ghosts sees something he thinks is the ghost of his dead wife, and the alien becomes that ghost. But ghosts have a precarious off-and-on existence. They are never quite of this world. Le Garrault even said that it was possible that some aliens kept shuttling back and forth between this world and the native world and were actually ghosts in both worlds.'

'Do you really expect me to believe that?' Childe said.

The baron puffed again and looked at the smoke as if it were a suddenly realized phantom. He said, 'No. Because I don't believe the ghost theory myself. Not as Le Garrault expounded it.'

'What do you believe then?'

'I really don't know,' the baron said, shrugging. 'Ghosts don't come from any universe I am familiar with. Their origin, their *modus operandi*, are mysterious. They exist. They can be dangerous.'

Childe laughed and said, 'You mean that vampires and werewolves, or whatever the hell they are, fear spooks?'

The baron shrugged again and said, 'Some fear them.'

Childe wanted to ask more questions but decided not to do so. He did not want the baron to know that he had found the room with the cameras and the Y-shaped table. It was possible that the baron intended to let him go, because he could dispose of the incriminating evidence before Childe could get the police here. For this reason. Childe did not ask him why Colben and Budler had happened to be his victims. Besides, it seemed obvious that Budler had been picked up by one of this group as a victim of their 'fun'. Magda or Vivienne or Mrs Krautschner, probably, had been the woman Colben had seen with Budler. And Colben, following Budler and the woman, had been detected and taken prisoner.

The baron rose and said, 'We might as well rejoin the others. From the sounds, I'd say the party is far from dead.'

117

Childe stood up and glanced at the open doorway, through which laughter and shrieks and hand-clapping spurted.

He jumped, and his heart lurched. Dolores del Osorojo was walking by the doorway. She turned her head and smiled at him and then was gone.

15

If the baron had seen her, he gave no sign. He bowed slightly and
gestured Childe to precede him. They went down the hall – no
Dolores anywhere – and were back in the dining room. O'Faithair
was playing wildly on the grand piano. Childe did not recognize the
music. The others were sitting at the table or on sofas or standing by
the piano. Glam and the two women had cleared off the table and
were carrying off the dishes from the sideboards. Mrs Grasatchow
was now drinking from a bottle of champagne. Magda Holyani was
sitting on an iron skeletal chair, her formal floor-length skirt pulled
up around her waist to expose her perfect legs to the suspender belt.
Dark-red hair stuck out from below the suspender belt. A half-
smoked marijuana cigarette was on the table by her side.

She was looking through an old-time stereoscope at a photograph.
Childe pulled her skirt down because the sight of her pubic hairs
bothered him and disgusted him, and he said, 'That's a curious
amusement for you. Or is the picture . . ?'

She looked up smiling, and said, 'Here. Take a look yourself.'

He placed the stereopticon against his eyes and adjusted the slide
holding the picture until the details became clear and in three
dimensions. The photograph was innocent enough. It showed three
men on a sail boat with a large mountain in the distant background.
The photograph had been taken close enough so that the features of
the men could be distinguished.

'One of them looks like me,' he said.

'That's why I got this album out,' she said. She paused, drew in
deeply on the marijuana, held the smoke in her lungs for a long
time and then puffed out. 'That's Byron. The others are Shelley and
Leigh Hunt.'

'Oh, really,' Childe said, still looking at the picture. 'But I
thought . . . I know it . . . the camera wasn't invented yet.'

'That's true,' Magda said. 'That's not a photograph.'

He did not get a chance to ask her to explain because two
enormous white arms went around him from behind and lifted him
off his feet. Mrs Grasatchow, shrieking with laughter, carried him to
a sofa and dropped him on it. He started to get up. He was angry
enough to hit her, and had his fist cocked, when she shoved him

back down again. She was not only very heavy; she had powerful muscles under the fat.

'Stay there, I want to talk to you and other things!' she said.

He shrugged. She sat down by him, and the sofa sank under her. She held his hand and leaned against him and continued the near-monologue she had been maintaining at the table. She told him of the men who had lusted after her and what she'd done to them. Childe was beginning to feel a little peculiar then. Things were not quite focused. He realized that he must be drugged.

A moment later, he was sure of it. He had seen the baron walk to the doorway and looked away for a second. When he looked back, he saw that the baron was gone. A bat was flying off down the hallway.

The change had taken place so quickly that it was as if several frames of film had been spliced in.

Or was it a change? There was nothing to have kept the baron from slipping off around the corner and releasing a bat. Or it was possible that there was, objectively, no bat, that he was seeing it because he had been drugged and because of the suggestions that Igescu was a vampire.

Childe decided to say nothing about it. Nobody seemed to have noticed it. They were not in shape to have noticed anything except what they were concentrating upon. O'Faithair was still playing madly. Bending Grass and Mrs Pocyotl were facing each other, writhing and shuffling in a parody of the latest dance. The redhead beauty, Vivienne Mabcrough, was sitting on another sofa with Rebecca Ngima, the beautiful Negress. Vivienne was drinking from a goblet in one hand while the other was slipped into the front of Ngima's dress. Ngima had her hand under Vivienne's dress. Pao, the Chinese, was on his back, his legs bent to support Magda, who was standing on his feet and getting ready to do a backward flip. She had taken off her shoes and dress and was clad only in her suspender belt, stockings, and net bra. She steadied herself and then, as Pao shoved upwards, soared up and over and landed on her feet. Childe thought that her unshod feet would have broken with the impact, but she did not seem to be bothered. She laughed and ran forward and did a forward flip over Pao and landed in front of a sofa on which Igescu's great-grandmother sat. The old woman reached out a claw and ripped off Magda's bra. Magda laughed and pirouetted away across the floor.

The baron had sauntered over to behind the baroness and had leaned over to whisper something to her. She smiled and cackled shrilly.

And then Magda ended her crazy whirl on Childe's lap. His head was pressed forward against her breasts. They smelled of a heady perfume and sweat and something indefinable.

Mrs Grasatchow shoved Magda so vigorously that she fell off Childe's lap and on to the floor. She looked up dizzily for a moment, her legs widespread to reveal the red-haired slit.

'He's mine!' Mrs Grasatchow shrilled. 'Mine! You snake-bitch!'

Magda got to her feet unsteadily. Her eyes uncrossed. She opened her mouth and her tongue flickered in and out and she hissed.

'Stay away!' Mrs Grasatchow said in a deeper voice. Had she really grunted?

Glam entered the room. He scowled at Magda. Evidently he did not like to see her in the almost-nude and making a play for Childe. But the baron froze him with a glare and motioned him to leave the room.

'Stay away, huh?' Magda said. 'You have no authority over me, pig-woman, nor am I afraid of you!'

'Pigs eat snakes,' Mrs Grasatchow replied. She grunted – yes, she grunted this time – and put one flesh-festooned arm over his shoulders and began to unzip his fly with the other hand.

'You've eaten everything and everybody else, but you haven't, and you aren't going to, eat this snake,' Magda said, spraying saliva.

Childe looked around and said, 'Where are the cameras?'

'Everything's impromptu tonight,' Mrs Grasatchow said. 'Oh, you look so much like George.'

Childe presumed that she meant George Gordon, Lord Byron, but he could not be sure and he did not care to play her game, anyway.

He pushed her hand away just as she closed two fingers on his penis, which, to his chagrin, was swelling. He felt nothing but repulsion for the fat woman, yet a part of him was responding. Or was it seeing Magda and also sharing in the general atmosphere of excitement? The drug, which he was sure he had been given, was basically responsible, of course.

Magda sat down on his lap again and put her arms around his neck. Mrs Grasatchow, snarling, raised her hand as if to strike Magda, but she let it drop when the baron called shrilly across the room. At that moment, a pair of large doors swung open. Childe, catching the movement at the corner of his eyes, turned his head. The baron was standing in the doorway. Behind him was *the* billiard room or *a* billiard room. It looked much like the first one he had seen. The two blondes, Chornkin and Krautschner, were playing.

The baron advanced across the room and, when a few paces behind Childe, said, 'The police don't know he's here.'

Childe erupted. He came off the sofa, tossing Magda away and then leaping over her and running towards the nearest door. He got to the hallway and was jerked violently off his feet, swung around, and pressed close to Glam. The great arms made him powerless to do anything except kick. And Glam must have been wearing heavy boots under his pants legs. Certainly he acted as if he did not feel the kicks. Perhaps he didn't. Childe may have had little strength.

As if he were a small child, he was led into the room. Glam holding his hand. The baron said, 'Good. Good for him and good for you. You restrained your impulse to kill him. Very commendable, Glam.'

'My reward?' Glam said.

'You'll get it. A share. As for Magda, if she doesn't want you, and she says she doesn't, she can continue to tell you to go to hell. My authority has its limits. Besides, you aren't really one of us.'

'You're lucky I haven't killed you, Glam!' Magda said.

'You have depraved tastes, Glam,' Mrs Grasatchow said. 'You'd fuck a snake if someone held its head, wouldn't you? I've offered you help . .'

'That's enough of that,' Igescu said. 'You two can play dice or a game of billiards for him. But the winner saves a piece for me, understood?'

'Dice won't take so long,' Magda said.

The baron nodded at Glam, who clamped a hand on Childe's shoulder from behind and steered him out of the room. Magda called, 'See you soon, lover!'

Mrs Grasatchow said, 'In a pig's ass, you will!' Magda laughed and said, 'He'll be in a pig's ass if you win!'

'Don't push me too far!' the fat woman shrilled.

Then Childe was being steered down the hall to its end and around the corner and down two flights of stairs. The hall here was of large grey blocks of stone. The door before which they halted was of thick black wood with iron bosses forming the outline of an archaic and grinning face. Glam shifted his grip from the shoulder to the neck and squeezed. Childe thought the blood would be pushed out of the top of his head. He went to his knees and leaned his head against the wall while his senses, and the pain in his neck, returned. Glam unlocked the door, dragged Childe into the room by one hand and dropped the hand when he came to the far wall. He completely undressed the feebly resisting Childe, lifted him up and snapped a metal collar shut around his neck. Glam picked up the clothes and went out, locking the door behind him.

There was a single unshaded light in the centre of the ceiling. The floor was covered with straw and a few blankets. The walls and ceiling were painted a light red.

When his strength came back, Childe found that the metal collar was attached by a four-foot long lightweight chain to an eyebolt sunk into the stone of the wall. He looked around but could see nothing to indicate that cameras or eyes were on him. The walls and ceiling seemed to be unbroken. However, it was possible that one or more of the stones was actually a one-way window.

There was a rattle at the door. A key clicked in the lock. The door swung open. Magda entered. She wore nothing unless you could count the key in her hand. She stood there smiling at him. Suddenly, she whirled. She said, 'Who is that?' and he got a glimpse of her back, of the egg-shaped hips, as she went swiftly into the hall.

There was a thump and a gasp. Then, silence.

Childe had no idea of what was happening, but he supposed that Glam or Grasatchow had attacked Magda. He had not thought that they would dare, since the baron had made it plain exactly how far they might go.

He waited. A sound as of a bare body being dragged along the stone floor came to him. Then, more silence. Then, a whispering. This sound was not that of a human voice but the friction of silk against silk.

He jerked with fright.

Dolores del Osorojo entered the doorway. With a swirl of skirts, she turned and closed the door. She faced him then and advanced slowly towards him, her white arms held out to him. She was not transparent or semi-opaque. She was as solid as young flesh could be. Her black hair and white face and red lips and white swelling bust were solid. And sweet.

Childe was too scared to respond to the arms around him and the breasts and lips pressed close to him. He was cold, although her breath was hot and the tongue she slid back and forth over his tongue was hot. Warm saliva leaked from her mouth over his chin and down his chest. She was panting.

Childe tried to back away. The wall stopped him. She pressed against him, and he lacked the will, or the strength, to try to push her away. He was still trembling.

The woman muttered something in Spanish. He did not understand the words, but her tone was intended to be soothing. She backed away and began to undress swiftly. The dress slid off, and the three petticoats, and then the knee length underwear and the long black stockings and corset. Dolores, in the nude, was a magnificent woman. The breasts were full and the nipples, almost as large as the ends of his thumbs, pointed upwards slightly. The pubic hair was thick and black and a line extended from it upward, like the smoke from a distant fire, to her navel. The fluid beginning to soak her hair and run down her leg showed how deeply impatient she was.

Childe, seeing these, felt less afraid. She looked too much of the protoplasm, too little of the ectoplasm, for him to believe to the core of his mind that she was truly a ghost.

He was far from being at ease, however. And when he tried his little Spanish to ask her if she could release him, he realized that she had no intention of letting him loose. Or else she was not able to do so.

He repeated his request that she get the key from Magda. She shook her head, indicating that she would not do so or she did not understand him. Perhaps – he hoped – she meant to release him but only after she had got what she wanted. What she wanted, for some reason or other, was Childe.

Not that it was any mystery about what she wanted. The reason why he was her choice was the mystery. At present, he could do nothing to find out.

She kissed him again and again and finally she began to play with his penis while she kissed him. He could not get an erection; the touch of her fingers turned his flesh cold as a dying man's and he shrank from her. He was, literally, spooked.

Finally, she quit kissing him. She backed away again and inspected him with stabs of her black eyes and then frowned. But she approached him again, speaking in soothing but incomprehensible Spanish, and got down on her knees in the straw. She took his limp penis into her warm mouth. She began to suck slowly, while the tips of her fingers touched the insides of his thighs where the thigh and belly met. His flesh began to warm, and the penis, as if the blood, once frozen, had suddenly become fluid, began to fill out. The old familiar but never boring sensations began to come back. He put his hands on her hair and pulled the high comb out and let it flood loose around her shoulders. He moved his hips back and forth.

Suddenly, she had unmouthed his penis and was kissing him again, running her tongue around his mouth. Then she took his penis and, rising to her toes, let herself down upon it. It slid up into her cunt; she moved back and forth a few times, and he came.

There are orgasms and there are orgasms.

This was so exquisite that he passed out, very briefly, during the ejaculations.

It was as if she had sparked within the chamber of her cunt, as if a century and a half of chastity were loosed along the shaft of his cock. Or as if she had generated a current that shot lightning down his nerves. So intense was the sensation, he was not sure that he was not burned out – literally. Perhaps something electrical *had been* discharged.

Childe was restricted to an upright position because of the chain. He told the woman, the ghost, or whatever she was, to get the key from Magda, but she paid him no attention except to look at him when he was talking. He could not understand why she did not get the key, since it was to her advantage to do so. And then it occurred to him that she was probably afraid that he would take off and leave her. And she did not want that, because she had too much to unloose. Or so it seemed to him.

He was limited in his area of activity and angle of position, but Dolores was ingenious. After she had sucked his penis into a full rigidity again, drawing in on it with just the reverse action of blowing up a balloon but with the direct effect of blowing and had licked off and swallowed the spermatic fluid and cleaned off his penis in the process, she released it. She got down on her hands and knees and turned away from him and then stood up on her hands, her legs spread wide. She let herself fall frontward, towards him, and her feet struck the wall on each side of him. After working her way forward on her hands a little, she was in a position she wanted. He thought at first of refusing her, but after considering that she might leave him locked up if he did, he grabbed her hips. His penis went past and under the anus and into the slit and she rocked back and forth.

Like Magda, she could squeeze and relax upon his penis with the muscles of the vaginal sheath. He moved only a little, pulling her hips in to him with short savage jerks. Within a few seconds, she was shuddering and sobbing, apparently having one orgasm on the heels of the next. Her cries were in Spanish. He knew little of that, but he could catch, 'Oh, holy fucking virgin mother Maria! Oh, father of the big cock! Fuck! Fuck! Shit! Shit! Oh, Christ, blessed Jesus, oh, sweet Jesus, he's fucking me! Fuck me, blessed flesh! Sweet flesh, fuck me!'

At that time he did not think about her words; he was just reacting. But he would remember and wonder. If she were the daughter of old Don del Osorojo, the sheltered daugther of the weird old grandee, she had a surprising vocabulary. But then, during a century and a half of hanging around live people, she could be expected to pick up words she might not have heard before death. But why hadn't she learned English in that time?

Now, he did not think of what she was saying. He was taking a long time coming, so long that he was able to turn her over, or around. Her arms were then braced below her, her feet against the wall, her cunt rammed against him, and she pushed back and forth while he reached down and rubbed her breasts and nipples with his hands. She had strong muscles; she could remain in that human-arch position, her head hanging down, and rock back and forth and occasionally stab her ass forward with no support of his hands under her hips.

After what seemed a long time, he jetted. Dolores screamed with the crescendo of climaxes. Then she let her feet slide down the wall while he helped ease her weight with his hands on her buttocks and then clamped her legs between his arms and let her slide on down. On the floor, she lay on her back, panting and looking up while spermatic fluid fell drop by drop into her open mouth. Then she scooted a little to one side to let the drops fall on her breasts and rubbed the sticky stuff over them. The chlorox odour of the fluid and the odour of sweat were strong in the chamber.

When her breathing became normal. Dolores rose and gave him a long tonguey spermaticky kiss. Her hand fondled his testicles.

He turned his head away and said, 'No more, Dolores. Or whoever or whatever you are.'

His legs trembled. Fucking in bed was demanding enough, but fucking standing up took twice as much out of him. And it seemed to him that Dolores had means for draining him of more than the normal quota of energy. For a few seconds, she had given him energy – he would swear that she had discharged a current down his penis – but then the orgasms had been so exquisite that they had opened the gates to drain the reservoir.

He had no objective reason for thinking so, but he *felt* that she had robbed him of a certain amount of vital energy and strengthened and solidified herself. Certainly, she had seemed flesh enough when he had felt her. But now, she seemed to have somehow become even more solid.

Dolores, seeing him shake so, said something, smiled, and held her finger up as if to tell him to wait there. (What the hell else could he do?) And she left the room. In a few seconds, she was back with a bottle of red wine and a big chunk of filet mignon. (Did she have quick and secret access to the kitchen?) He said no to the wine but eagerly ate the meat. Although he had finished supper only a half-hour ago, or so it seemed, he was very hungry.

Dolores tilted the bottle to her lips and drank. Almost, he expected to see a dark column going down the throat and into the stomach, as if she were a transparent figure in a stomach-acid commercial. But he could see only the Adam's apple moving.

If he was hungry, she was thirsty. She kept the bottle to her lips until it was half empty. She may have intended to fully empty it, but a noise came through the door, which she had left ajar. Dolores jerked and dropped the bottle. It fell on its side and spurted red wine on the straw.

She bent down and scooped up all her clothes, rolled them into a bundle, which she placed under her right arm, and then kissed him swiftly, breathing wine and sperm. She ran to the wall on his right; her left hand pushed along the juncture of two grey blocks. With a groan and a squeak, a section of wall, consisting of blocks six high and four wide, swung inward on the left side. The interior was dark. Dolores turned and smiled and threw something that glittered. He lunged for it, but the chain jerked him back, cutting off his breath, and the object bounced off his fingertips and fell on the straw.

It was the key to the lock on the metal collar.

The darkness swallowed Dolores. The section, squeaking and groaning again, swung shut.

A huge head with huge jowls, large purplish eyes, and a high-piled blue-black hairdo, came around the corner of the doorway. Mrs Grasatchow.

127

From behind her came excited voices. The fat woman's eyes widened. She pushed the door open and waddled across the straw to Childe. He slowly drew back the foot he had extended to try to move the key towards him.

Mrs Grasatchow sniffed loudly and then screamed. 'Jism!' She grunted like a sow about to give birth. 'Who's been here? Who? Tell me! Who?'

'Didn't you see her?' Childe said. 'She went down the hall!'

'Who?'

'Dolores del Osorojo!'

Mrs Grasatchow's skin was naturally pale and made even whiter by her powder. But she managed to turn more white.

The baron, a long cigar in one hand, entered the room. He said, 'I thought it would be Dolores. Only she . . .'

The fat woman whirled swiftly, as graceful as a rhinoceros, which is huge but can be very graceful in certain movements.

'You said . . . you pooh-poohed Dolores! You said she couldn't be any danger to us!'

The baron looked shrewdly at Childe before answering. He puffed on his cigar, and said, 'It didn't seem likely that she would ever get enough plasm long enough to harden it. But I was wrong.'

'What did she do to Magda?' Mrs Grasatchow said.

The baron shrugged. 'We'll have to ask Magda that when she comes to. If she does.'

The doorway was filled with the body of Glam. He carried Magda, still naked, in his arms. Her head lolled, her long blonde hair hung down, her arms and legs were limp.

Glam said, 'What do I do with her?'

'Take her upstairs to her room. Put her to bed. Tell Vivienne to look at her.'

Glam's expression flickered from stone-mask to something unreadable, and back to stone-mask. The baron said, 'She's defenceless now, true. But if I were you, I wouldn't try anything.'

Glam said nothing. He turned and carried the woman off. The two blonds, Chornkin and Krautschner, looked in, each from a side of the doorway.

'Did you see Dolores?' the baron said.

They shook their heads. The baron glanced at the section of wall which had opened for Dolores. He opened his mouth as if he were going to tell the two where she had gone and to send them after her.

But he closed his lips.

Childe thought that perhaps the baron preferred to keep certain secrets. Didn't he trust the two? Or did he think it would be futile to chase after her? In any event, he must think that Childe had seen the exit.

'She has to be flesh enough to fuck,' Mrs Grasatchow said. 'Look at the redness of his cock and the jism.'

'I can see,' the baron said dryly. 'Magda's key was gone. Childe, do you have it?'

Childe shook his head. Igescu went to the two young people and they whispered for a moment. Then they turned their backs to each other and went off down the hall, bent over, searching. The baron came back in and said, 'Take your eyes off his cock, and help me look for that key.'

'Here it is!' Mrs Grasatchow said.

She stooped, picked it up, and straightened, groaning. The baron took it and put it in his jacket pocket.

Childe tightened his lips. He had no chance now, unless Dolores came back to help him. He doubted that she would. Although she had thrown the key to him, she had not made sure he had had it, and she had had time to do so. The gesture had seemed to say that he could escape if he were agile enough and clever enough. Perhaps she was resentful of her long, long frustrating imprisonment in incorporeality. She might have wanted him to suffer, too. After all, she had taken him, not because of affection or love but because she needed an object to relieve herself on.

But she was partly on his side. That was his only hope, at present.

The baron left the room, and, in a few seconds, the young people entered. The boy had the key. He unlocked the collar, and he and the girl, each holding Childe by an arm, hustled him out of the room. They passed two doors and entered the third, which was already open. This was a room the size of the one he had just left, but the walls were oak-panelled, the ceiling was painted light blue, and the floor was covered with a thick Persian rug with swastikas inside circles. There were a number of collars hanging from chains attached to bolts sunk into the wall, however. Childe was again held by a metal collar.

This room must have no secret entrances.

The baron looked at his wristwatch and said, 'We have to do something about her. She wasn't dangerous until she got enfleshed.

But everything has its disadvantage. Now she's dangerous, she's also vulnerable. We can do something about her, and we will. I'm going to call a conference.'

Mrs Grasatchow pouted. She said, 'Now Magda's out of the way, I'd thought . . .'

'Half an hour. No more,' Igescu said. 'I'll send somebody down to escort you. You wouldn't want to be alone on the way up.'

The fat woman started. It was as if a tidal wave were racing through her flesh.

'You mean *I* . . . *I* . . . have to worry? That *I'm* in danger?' She bellowed with laughter.

'We all are,' the baron said. 'All of a sudden, our security is gone. This,' he stabbed a thumb at Childe, 'has something to do with it but I don't know what. He's a focus of some sort. Maybe Dolores has been waiting for someone like him all these years.

'Half an hour,' he said. 'I mean it. And don't use him up. I still want a piece of him.'

The baron left, closing the door behind him. Mrs Grasatchow started to take her clothes off. Childe's legs began to shake again.

16

He told her that she was wasting her time. He did not tell her that, even if he had not been drained and weakened, he would have been unable to respond positively to her. The enormous hanging breasts, the tremendous belly, which curved out and overhung the genitals so far that they could not be seen in the shadows and folds, the hips, sackish with fat, the tree-trunk legs, repulsed him. He doubted that he could have got a hard-on even if he were in full strength and had not had an emission for a month.

Mrs Grasatchow said, 'That spook-bitch sucked you dry, heh?' And then she laughed. She was close to him; the blast of alcohol made him feel like vomiting. There must be almost two gallons in that pony-sized gut.

She had brought into the room a large bearskin-purse and a bottle of wine and a bottle of Scotch. She poured the wine over his belly and genitals and then got on her knees and licked them off. He did not respond.

She came up off her knees like a boulder tossed up by a volcanic explosion. Her hand struck him on the side of his jaw. He saw comets and fell back, half-conscious, against the wall.

'You little asshole!' she screamed. 'You may look like George, but you sure aren't the man he was!'

She waddled to her purse and took out a silvery cone about two inches long. 'This will put some life into you! Once it's in you!'

Grinning, she approached him. He shrank back against the wall and then leaped out at her, striking at her. Laughing, she caught his wrist and turned it until he cried out in agony and sank to his knees as far as the chain would allow. Choking, he tried to stand up again, but she forced him down until he was almost unconscious again.

He regained his senses to find himself turned around, his face to the wall. Something – he knew it was the cone – was being shoved up his anus.

'You've never had anything like this, little man!' she crooned. 'Never! You'll not forget this night, as long as you live. Oh, little man, I wish I were you just now, so I could fuck me!'

The cone burned at first and made him feel as if he had to shit. After about half a minute, it seemed to turn icy and to become heavy, as if it were a lead sinker just removed from a freezer. The coldness and heaviness spread out, up his intestines, coil after coil, like a snake racing ahead of the Ice Age but too slow, into his testicles, which became bells ringing with chilliness, into his solar plexus, and, at the other terminus, into his penis. Liquid nitrogen pumping into every tube of his body.

He squirmed as the stuff fell down the shafts of his legs and flapped slowly spiralling up the shaft of his trunk. The powerful hands of the fat woman tightened, and she said, 'Quiet, little lover. This won't hurt you, and you'll be a man such as you never were!'

The icy weight lapped at the base of his brain. His neckbones and hindbrain felt crystallized. He could distinguish each vertebra and each cell of the cerebellum as a frozen entity. He could also feel the individual vessels of his penis slowly filling with half-frozen blood. By then, Mrs Grasatchow had turned him around again and was down on her elephantine knees and sucking on his penis. She grunted as if she were a sow tearing into a corncob, but, as far as he could detect, he was being treated gently enough. Her jaws did not move, only her lips, shaped around the glans, moved. He could feel nothing. He might as well have had a hundred local shots of morphine over his body and one massive shot in his penis. But if his brain was receiving no tactile message, part of his body was. The penis, like an independent creature, a leech stuck in her mouth and drawing blood from her tongue, was gradually filling up.

When she felt that it was as swollen and rigid as it could be, she stood up. She said, 'You're not going any place, not now!' She unlocked the collar and put the key in her purse. He tried to run from her to the door, but his legs would not move.

She lay down on the floor and spread her thighs open – it was like the Red Sea splitting to make passage for the horde of Moses – and she said, 'Eat me!'

Obediently, although his frozen brain tried to push out a message of resistance to his nerves, he got down and spread the slit open and prepared to tongue the clitoris first, as was his habit.

She said, 'No, idiot! The other way! Sixty-nine!'

He crawled up on to her and swivelled around. She took in his penis until his hairs pressed against her lips. He could not feel this, but he looked through the space that existed briefly between their bodies and saw the hairs and the narrow band of the root. He flicked the tip of his tongue over the 'little penis'. A 'little penis' this clitoris was. He had never seen such an enormous one. He did have some difficulty getting to it, however, because her belly was so huge. It was like having to curve over a hill, hanging upside down, to lick at a spring in a crevasse at the bottom of the hill.

The worst of it was, he felt no sexual stimulation, only disgust. But he had to do exactly as she said, and his organs, outside of the brain, must be responding to some sensory input.

At another order, he withdrew his penis from her mouth and turned around and inserted his penis into her vagina. He began pumping slowly but soon speeded up in response to her command. She began groaning and moaning, turning her head from side to side, crying out in a foreign language, rolling the great hips sideways and then thrusting and now and then lifting herself up from the waist and grabbing his buttocks and pulling and pushing him.

He did not know how long they were in this position nor whether or not he had an orgasm. But the time came when she rolled him off her, the uncoupling wetly announced itself, and got above him and eased herself down upon his penis and moved the great body as lightly and swiftly as a toy balloon on the end of a string. After what seemed to be a hundred orgasms, judging by her number of frenzies, she got off him and went to the corner after her bottle of whisky. He seemed able to move a little on his own volition, so he turned to watch her. She sat on the rug, leaning against the wall, looking like an over-yeasted mass of dough.

Childe became aware that he was gasping. He could hear his breath rattling in and out, but he could not feel the thudding of his heart nor the moving of his ribs.

Mrs Grasatchow downed at least a fourth of the quart and then looked at her wristwatch.

'Forty-five minutes,' she said. 'Igescu will be furious.'

She heaved herself up and said, 'Hmm! What's wrong? He said he'd send somebody after me.'

She opened the door and looked down the hallway. Childe tried to run towards her then, hoping to knock her down with his momentum and get away down the hall. He only managed, after a seemingly long time, to get to his feet. If he had exerted himself prodigiously, he did not know it. Reception from his muscles was still cut off.

On seeing him move, the woman's eyebrows went up, and she said, 'Do you feel that suppository burning now?'

'No,' he said. 'It's still cold and heavy.'

'You'll feel it in a moment. You'll think a hot-air balloon is going up your ass!'

A laughquake shook her. Afterward, she said, 'That stuff has a very peculiar effect. You didn't feel anything while you were fucking me, but wait. I wish I could take advantage of you then, but you'll have to enjoy yourself with yourself.'

She looked at her wristwatch again. 'Maybe I won't go. I think Igescu has forgotten me. Or he knows I'll be very angry indeed if I don't get all of you. Now, you just stand right there, little Georgey Porgey Pudding and Pie. I'll fix you up again, and double the effect. I don't want you acting up on me.'

As if a bore tide had reversed and was running back to sea, the coldness and heaviness became warmth and lightness. The second effect started where the first had ended, in the brain and the tip of his glans. The warmth and lightness raced inward from all borders and met in the region of the cone, in his anus, where, for a second, it burned as if a meteorite had just ended its fiery curve there.

He cried out with the pain.

The fat woman said, 'Oh, oh! It's happened!' and she charged, one hand open to grab him and another cone in the other hand. She seemed to grow as large as the wall. Her flesh shook like a loose robe in a stiff wind. Childe launched himself at her, his hands out to grab her ears, because he meant to tear them off. He would have to fight savagely to get past her to the door. Even when he had his full strength, he would have been out-muscled by her, not to mention outweighed.

His hands caught her ears, and his face thrust into one breast as violently as if he had been dropped from the ceiling on to her. She screamed, because he had bitten down on the excrescence suddenly appearing between his teeth. It was her nipple, as he found out when he got up from the floor where she had thrown him. He spat out the piece of flesh – the nipple and some white skin around it – and rose shakily. She was still screaming and rolling back and forth and clutching her mutilated breast.

Childe did not wait to completely recover from the impact of the floor. Fighting dizziness and a pain in his shoulder, he kicked her between her legs as she started to roll towards him. His big toe disappeared momentarily in her slit. She screamed again. A flailing arm knocked his leg out from under him. He fell crosswise on top of her belly. She clamped her arms down on his buttocks and then one hand slid down to grab his testicles. With a desperate jerk, he turned over to face her, still crosswise, seized a breast, and twisted.

Her arms came up; she screamed again. Childe rolled away across her belly and down her legs. It was like rolling down a small hill. He got out of the way of her kicking legs and leaped up and came down with both bare feet on her face. Her head was driven back against the floor; her nose smashed; blood burst; her eyes crossed.

Again, he leaped and came down with both feet on her belly. He sank deep. Her wind whooshed out, as if somebody had opened a big door to a distillery with a strong crossdraught. He almost gagged. But he jumped a third time, once more on her face. Her nose became even flatter. Her eyes rolled up until only the whites showed. Her mouth was wide open, braced like a sail against the wind of her agony to get her breath back.

And, at that moment, the cone reversed its effect. It was as if the entire coition with her had been recorded with a glass window between himself and his nerve endings. He could see but could not hear. Now, the glass was gone, and he could hear the rerun. With this difference. He was no longer frozen. He now felt everything exquisitely; he could feel his cock in her mouth and between her breasts and in her cunt, even though they were no longer there.

During the fight, though he had not been aware of it, he had had an erection. Now, he jetted, and the delayed reaction orgasm stormed his body. He fell to the floor and writhed helplessly, if ecstatically in its lightnings. There was nothing else, for the moment, he could do.

17

When he could regain control, he got up and staggered towards the door. Although his penis no longer spouted, it remained as hard as before and did not have the delicious emptied-to-good-purpose feeling of an after-orgasm. It did feel pleasurable, increasingly pleasurable, as if he were again working up to coition. He could, however, ignore it for the present.

Mrs Grasatchow still lay on her back, arms and legs outflung, her mouth open, and her eyes open and showing white, as if hardboiled eggs had been stuffed into the sockets.

He noticed a large turd spread out on the rug between him and Mrs Grasatchow. So, he had been 'scared shitless' sometime during the fight. He had not known when he spurted out the excrement; it did not matter. He was sure he had expelled the turd and not she, although it was possible that she had when he had jumped on her face. It was, however, so far from her that he doubted it.

Gingerly stepping by the turd, he walked to her purse, which was near the door. In it he found the key to the door. She had locked the door after looking down the hallway the last time. He unlocked it and, carrying her purse, went down the hall towards the room in which he had been originally imprisoned.

First, though he hated the idea of any delay, he had to investigate the other rooms along the hall. There was always the chance of other prisoners there. Perhaps Sybil was in one. Six doors were closed. Three were unlocked and contained not much of interest. Three opened to the key from the fat woman's purse.

The first two were small rooms with padded walls and floor. The third contained some furniture, modern Danish, with a colour TV set, a well-stocked bar, a pool table, and cartons of cigarettes and cigars and boxes of marijuana sticks and bottles with pills of various sizes, shapes, and colours. It looked as if it might be a rest room or recreation room. The occupants could relax here between their working bouts in the other room. There was also a large bureau with a mirror, which he did not think was one-way. The top of it was crowded with cosmetics and held some wigs.

He opened the drawers, hoping to find some clothes he could wear. Before he could examine one, he was overcome with another semi-epileptic orgasm and jetted over the clothes in the top drawer. There was a wash room which he used to clean his genitals, face and hands, and his mouth. He drank several glasses of water and returned to the bureau.

There were some T-shirts and gym shorts. He found some that were near enough to his size and put them on. Then it occurred to him that he was going to have another ejaculation soon and would be very uncomfortable. It was either that or stick his cock out. He decided on the latter, although he felt ridiculous. And he looked ridiculous in the mirror. A knight with a stubby delicate lance. Some knight! Some detective! A private dick become public.

There were some socks but no shoes. He put the socks on and continued his search. If only a weapon were here. No luck. Too much to hope for, of course. The two lower drawers were crammed with flat transparent plastic envelopes containing something unidentifiable. He opened one and shook out the contents. It fluttered out like a transparent flag to a length of about six feet. It had four extensions, a thick mass of hair on one end, and a circular mass of hair in the middle. Just beside the thick mass of hair was a small red valve like that on a child's plastic inflatable swimming pool. He blew it up and felt weakened by the exertion before he had completed the job.

After seeing what he had, he was horrified, although he had suspected what the result would be.

Somehow, Colben's skin had been stripped from his body and made into a balloon. The apertures: earholes, mouth, anus, and the mutilated penis, had been sewn over with flaps of skin. His eyes had been painted blue, and the mouth was painted with a facsimile of labial red. The pubic hairs were still attached, and these, together with the sewed fold between his legs, gave him a womanish appearance.

Childe did not have time to deflate him. He pushed him sailing away, and frantically removed the contents of the other envelopes. One was the head of Budler. He presumed that the wolf in the film had eaten the rest of Budler or so mangled it that it could not be used for a balloon. His head went spinning over and over towards the corner, where Colben, turned upside down by the weight of his hair, and the valve on the back of his neck, stood on his head.

There were a number of women, only four of whom had the right length or colour of hair for Sybil. Despite this, he inflated all of them. When he had blown up the last one, he was panting as if he had run a half-mile through the smog. The effort was only partly responsible. He had been so certain that the last one would have Sybil's features.

He sat down and sipped on another glass of water. There were thirty-eight skins at one end of the room. Most of them were upside down, but a few had fallen against the others and leaned one way or another. The light from a lamp in the corner shone through many of them so that they seemed a mob of drunken ghosts. The draught from the air-conditioning moved them back and forth a little so that they also seemed like phantoms of the drowned.

Thirty-eight. Twenty-five males. Thirteen females. Of the males, fifteen were Caucasians, seven were Negroes, three were Mongolians or Indians. Of the females, nine were Caucasians and four were Negresses.

All were adults. If any had been children, he would not have been able to endure it. He would have run screaming down the hall. He thought he was tough, but he would not have been able to stand the sight of the inflated skins of children.

As it was, he was angry and sick. More angry than sick at the moment. What were they planning on doing with these . . . these corpse-balloons? Fill them with hydrogen and send them flying over Los Angeles?

That was probably exactly what they did plan on doing. It would be on a par with, no, would surpass, the effrontery of the films.

He rose and took a bottle of vodka by the neck and went back to the doorway of the room in which he had left Mrs Grasatchow. She was sitting up and vomiting. Blood was still trickling from her nostrils. On seeing Childe, she snarled and managed to lift herself to her feet. Blood and vomit smeared her immense belly.

'You'll beg me to kill you!' she screamed.

'Why will I?' he said. He stepped inside the room. 'Before I kill you, I want you to tell me why you did that to all those people? And why did you strip off their skins?'

'I'll rip your balls off!' she shouted. She charged him then; he braced himself, the bottle lifted high. But she stepped on the turd and her feet shot up and ahead of her and she fell heavily on her back. She lay there, groaning but seemingly knocked out. He hit her, once, on the side of her head with the bottle she had dropped and then locked the door to the room. The bottle in one hand and her purse on the other arm, and his penis sticking out – what a hero I make! he thought – he entered the room in which he had first been chained.

But he came out of it at once and went into the recreation room. He needed evidence. The police wouldn't believe much of his story after he told it, but they would have to believe that a part of it was true when he showed them Colben and Budler. And another picked at random who might turn out to have been reported missing.

The deflation was as ghastly as he had expected. The air hissed out, and Budler and the woman shrank like the witch on whom Dorothy had thrown water. But Colben – he always was slippery – got away and shot around the room, butting into several of the phantoms and knocking them head over heels. He came to rest draped over the bar. Childe pulled him off the bar then as he had pulled him away several times when he was living. He rolled him up and stuffed him into the purse on top of Budler's head and the red-headed woman.

The section of wall opened for him after a number of experiments of running his hand along the juncture of the blocks which Dolores had pressed. He stepped inside with a pencil-flashlight taken from the purse. The section swung shut behind him, and he began walking slowly. The passage way was warm and dusty and narrow. It led past several rooms, each of which had a one-way mirror but no entrance that he could detect. They were similar to those lining the other hallway. A stairway confronted him. He walked up this uneasily, although he did not think that it could be a trap, since he was deep in the earth. But he could not be sure. At the top, he was in a passageway which offered him two routes. There were prints in the dust, a long pointed shoeprint which he presumed was the baron's and those of a dog or a wolf. The latest led to the right, so he decided to follow them. One way was as good as another, and something had to decide him.

His flashlight showed him several squares in the walls. When he opened these, he saw through one-way mirrors into a number of rooms, one of which he thought he remembered. It was a Louis Quatorze bedroom, but it did not seem quite like the one he remembered. It did have an entrance through the panelling. He took it and after stepping softly around it and looking into the bathroom, knew this was not the same room. The queer disturbing mirror was missing. He started to open the door to look out into the next room or the hallway but thought better of it. He placed his ear against the wood and was glad that he had done so. The murmur of voices came through the wood.

The keyhole let him hear more clearly but not clearly enough.

After turning off all the lights in the room, he turned the knob carefully and eased the door open. The voices came from the end of the hall. He could see partway down it but not far enough to see the speakers. The voices were identifiable, except for two. These could be Chornkin's and Krautschner's since they had not spoken when introduced or at the dinner table. They could also be those of newcomers.

'. . . much energy from Magda, as I said before,' Igescu was saying loudly. He seemed exasperated and, perhaps, a little frightened. 'I think Dolores had gathered enough around her to take a tangible and enduring shape, enough to render Magda powerless for a moment and suck her almost dry. She didn't kill Magda but she came damn close. And then Glam, that damn fool! He deserved what he got! But then what can you expect from his kind? Glam fucked her, although I'd warned him often enough what might happen. I think he thought he was safe. But the very act of fucking gave her energy enough; she came to and found Glam in her, how she hated him! And you saw Glam!'

The strange male voice interrupted softly. Childe could not understand what he was saying. Igescu's reply was loud enough.

'Yes, Magda got the energy but not enough! She's stuck in stasis, and she won't get out unless she kills another! Which will mean someone here, in this house!'

The strange female voice spoke then; it was even softer than the male's. Igescu said, 'Childe would do it! I had other plans for him, but I can give them up! We have to find Magda first and get her to Childe! Otherwise . . !'

'Dolores?' Mrs Pocyotl said.

Childe could almost see the baron's shrug. The baron said, 'Who knows? She's X! A dangerous X! If she can do that to Magda, she can do that to any of us. But I doubt that she could attack more than one of us at a time and I think she'd have to surprise us, just as she must have surprised Magda! So, we'd better hang together, as . . .'

A shout interrupted him. Footsteps sounded. The group was going around the corner and down the stairs to the cause of commotion. More shouts. He swung the door wider and peeped down the hall. The only one there was Bending Grass, who leaned his stocky form against the wall and cocked his head to look down the stairway. Then somebody called his name and he disappeared.

Childe ran down the hallway to the only door opened. This was by the head of the steps, and the group had been assembled outside it. He stuck his head in. The room was strange, looked more like a movie director's idea of a Turkish harem than anything else. There were rugs and drapes and cushions and ottomans and even a hookah and a dresser so low that Magda must have had to sit crosslegged while she looked in the mirror. There was a marble-lined bath sunk level with the floor. It was almost large enough to qualify as a small swimming pool. Beyond it was a low marble enclosure which presumably had served Magda as a bed, since it was piled with cushions and pillows and canopied with many silk veils.

Glam's black soft-leather boots stuck out over the enclosure. Childe walked swiftly in, past the bath, which was full of cold water, and looked over the marble railing. Glam had died with his boots on. Also, his pants. He had stripped off his shirt and undershirt and pulled his pants down around his knees, but he had been too eager to bother taking all his clothes off.

There was blood on his pants and much blood on his body. Blood had spurted out from his ears, nostrils, eyes, mouth, anus, and penis. Something had violently squeezed him. The ribs were caved in; the arms were flattened; the hip bones had been pushed inward towards each other. Not only blood had been expelled from every aperture. The contents of the bowels and about six feet of the bowels themselves had been pressed out of his anus.

Near the bed, a section of wall stood open. Whether Magda had taken this or Igescu had opened it to see if she had taken it, Childe could not know. But he could not linger long here; his route of escape was suddenly no longer a matter of choice. Voices announced the return of the others. He might have had time to slip back through the door and up the hallway, but he did not dare chance it. He went through the opening in the wall.

Before he had taken a dozen steps, he was seized. He groaned with a despairing ecstasy and braced himself with both hands against the walls while he spouted and shook. Afterwards, he cursed, but he could do nothing about his condition. He walked on. His penis still stuck straight out and slightly at an upward angle, like the bowsprit of a ship. The cone was working within him. God knew how long its effect lasted, how long it would take to melt entirely away.

Almost, he decided to hide in the passageway near the still open panel and eavesdrop. But every second he was in this house meant recapture or death, and he was frightened because of what had happened to Glam and of what the others had said about Magda. Frightened was not strong enough. He was close to panic. And this was strange, because the terror should have taken from him any sexual stimulation whatsoever. Under these circumstances, he should have been unable to retain an erection. But there it was, independent of his other feelings, as if a switch had been thrown to place his genitals on a separate circuit. The cone, whatever it was, must not only be the prime mover of his state, it must also be the prime feeder. It had to be furnishing the energy to keep manufacturing all this spermatic fluid at such an extraordinary – for him – rate of speed. Generally, when unusually stimulated, when first in love, or sometimes when the marijuana hit him just right, he could have three or four orgasms within several hours. But, usually, one or two in an hour, and he was done for four or five hours. He had sometimes twitted himself with being the most undersexed private eye in history, without, of course, really believing his self-deprecation. But now, he seemed to be a fountain with a never-ending reservoir. And, of course, he *would* be so in a situation where it was the last thing he wanted.

Thus, when he thought he was far enough away from the panelling, he turned on the flashlight. And he saw the white figure of Dolores coming towards him. Her arms were open and she was smiling. Her eyes were half-lidded but bright, and two patches of wetness shone on her thighs. It seemed to be his misfortune to encounter overlubricating women. However, after a century and a half of enforced abstinence, she could not be blamed.

She barred his way. She was solid flesh enough, no man knew that better than he, yet he hesitated to attack her. The fate of Magda was warning enough. Moreover, there was the chance that if he did what she wanted, he might work off the effect of the cone. It was just possible. And he thought that he probably had no choice, anyway. So he put down his purse, turned off the flashlight, and dropped his pants. She pulled him down on her and he put his penis in swiftly and began to thrust without preliminaries of any kind. He had hoped that he would come at once, but even though he now had her soft wet flesh around his penis, and though the pleasure was somewhat heightened, he was unable to disengage himself from the automatic effects of the cone.

At length he came and then, when he tried to pull himself away, he found himself unable to. Her arms looked feminine and soft enough and felt so, but she had the strength of a python in each.

Thinking of pythons made him think of Magda, and he became even more alarmed. If she came upon them now, she would have him helpless . . . those coils . . . Glam . . . He shuddered even as he began to pump again. His skin had turned cold and his hairs felt as if they were bristling in the static of terror. His anus was a dot of ice, a bull's eye for Magda if she crawled up behind him and raised her head to unloose a hammer stroke.

He groaned and muttered, 'I must be out of my mind, I'm really believing that crap!' and then he groaned again, this time because he was coming once more.

It was no use. Lying with Dolores was not cancelling or even diminishing the effects of the cone. And he was certainly not stupid enough to bang away at her for the sheer pleasure of it while his life was in danger. Especially since he had had enough of this 'pleasure' to last him for a long time.

He tried to break loose. Her arms did not tighten, but they also did not relax. He was not going to get out until he had satisfied her or was unable to keep an erection, and she was not going to be satisfied for a long time and he did not know how long he would last, but he suspected that he would last for hours and hours.

Remembering what he had done to Mrs Grasatchow during the fight, he bit down upon Dolores' nipple. His bite did not take the nipple off, but it was painful enough to cause her to open her arms and to scream. He was out of her embrace and had jumped away to where she could not reach him, pulling up his pants, stooped to pick up the flashlight and purse, and was running down the passageway, before she had stopped screaming.

The noise, of course, would be heard in Magda's room if the panelling were still open, and they would be investigating. His flashlight beam bounded up and down and then went off into darkness at a corner. He stopped and probed around. Apparently, he was at a dead end, but he did not believe it. Shouts behind him sent him into a frenzy of tapping and poking against the wall to activate whatever mechanism moved this section. He felt somebody brush his shoulder, somebody spoke in Spanish, and a white arm reached past him and touched a cornice. Another arm pushed in on another cornice. The blank wall became a blank darkness in which the thin beam was lost. A hand pushed him on through – he seemed to be paralysed for a few seconds – and then he turned just in time to see the section swing back into place. Beyond, the beam from a large flashlight flicked into existence.

A hand, still greasy from playing with his penis, slipped in his and the white figure led him down a passageway and up a flight of steps. The dust was thick here; he sneezed resoundingly several times, Igescu would have no trouble following them because of their newly made footprints. They had to get out of the secret ways, for a while, anyway.

Dolores, whose footprints were as clear as his, seemed to realize that they betrayed them. She stopped before a wall, unfastened several latches and slid back the section. They stepped into a room with grey-and-white marble walls, red marble ceiling, black-and-red marble floor, and furniture of white or black marble. The chandelier was a mobile composed of thin curved pieces of coloured marble with sockets for candles.

Dolores led him across the room. She had dropped his hand and her right hand was pressed against her breast, which must hurt very much. Her face was expressionless, but the hot black eyes seemed to promise him revenge. If she had wanted it, she could have abandoned him in the passageway, he thought. Perhaps she, wanted to take revenge personally.

He caught a glimpse of them as they passed a tall mirror. They looked like two lovers who had been interrupted in bed and who were fleeing a jealous husband. She was naked, and his penis, still wet and tipped with a globule of spermatic fluid, was projecting from his fly. They looked comical enough; the purse added an incongruous, doubtful, touch.

There was nothing comical about the pack behind them. He crowded on Dolores' heels and urged her to go faster. She said something and half-ran through the door and down and down a luxurious hall with thick carpeting. Near the end of the hall, by a curving stairway with marble steps and a carved mahogany handrail, she pushed open another door. There was a suite of four rooms done in opulent Edwardian style. The bedroom contained the entrance to the intramural passageway; a bookcase slid aside to reveal an iron gate of two sections locked by a combination lock. Dolores turned the knob swiftly as if she had much practice with it. The two sections of gate could then be pushed aside. When they were on the other side, she pushed them together and spun the combination dial on this side. Apparently, this action activated a mechanism, because the bookcase slid back into place. The light through the opening had shown him that they were not in a passageway but in a small room. Cool air moved past him. Dolores turned on a lamp. He saw several chairs, a bed, a TV set, a bar, a dresser with mirror, books, and cabinets. The cabinets held cans of food and delicacies; one cabinet was the door to a well-stocked refrigerator. A door off the room led to a bathroom and a closet full of clothes. Igescu could hide here for a long time if he wished.

Dolores spoke in Spanish, slowly. He understood the simple sentence. 'Here we are safe for a while.'

'About my biting you, Dolores,' he said. 'I had to. I must get out of here.'

She paid him no attention. She looked at her breast in the mirror and murmured something. Teethmarks and a red aureole ringed the nipple. She turned and shook her finger at him and then smiled, and he understood that she was gently reprimanding him for being overpassionate. He must not bite her again. After which warning, she took his hand and pulled him towards the bed.

He lunged away, tearing loose from her grip, and said, 'Nothing doing! Show me the way out of here! *Vámanos! Pronto!*'

He began to inspect the walls. She spoke slowly behind him. Her words were clear and simple enough. If he would stay for a little, he would be shown the way out. But no more biting.

'No more nothing,' he said. He found the control, a piece of corner carving which could be moved on a pivot. The dresser moved out on one side. He went through while Dolores yelled at him from the room. She sounded so much like Sybil giving him hell, although he understood not a word, that he was able to ignore her. He carried a sharp-edged rapier, one of a set on the wall, in one hand and the flashlight in the other. The handle of the purse was over his left shoulder. The blade gave him confidence. He did not feel so helpless now. In fact, if he got a chance, he would leave the passageway and walk out the front door and if they got in his way, they would get the blade where it would do them the least good and him the most.

The way out did not come easily, however. The passageway ran into a stairway which led steeply upward into the shadows. He backtracked to look for one-way windows or entrances to rooms but could find no unlocking controls. So he returned to the stairway, which he walked up with as little weight on his feet as possible. He stuck the sword through his belt and held the flashlight in his teeth while he braced his arms against the walls. If the stairway straightened out, it would not drop him down a chutey-chute.

The stairs held, and he was on a narrow landing. The door was easily opened by a conventional knob. He stepped cautiously out into a curving-walled room with a great window lit by the moon, a dim pale eye in the haze. Looking through the window, he saw the yard and trees and driveway at the front of the central portion. He was in the cupola on the left wing, just beside the original Spanish building. It contained three rooms, two of which were empty. The door to the third was part way open, and light streamed through it. He crouched by it and slowly extended his head, then had to withdraw it while he shook and spurted and clenched his teeth and clamped his lips to keep from groaning.

18

Afterwards, he looked through the doorway again. The baron's great-grandmother was sitting on a high stool before a high table with a sloping top, such as old-time bookkeepers (Bob Cratchit) used when they wrote accounts (for Ebenezer Scrooge). He could not see what was on the table except that it was a large paper of some sort. Her jaws were moving, and now and then he could hear something but could not tell if the words were English or not. The only light was from a single lamp suspended from the ceiling directly overhead. It dimly showed walls with large, thick, black painted symbols, none of which he recognized; a long table with racks of bottles containing fluids; a globe of Earth with all sorts of curlicues painted in thin lines over it, sitting at the end of the table; a large birdcage on a stand in one corner with a raven, its head stuck under a wing; and a robe hanging on a hook on the wall.

After a few minutes of muttering, the baroness got down off the stool. Her bones snapped and creaked, and he did not think she would make it to the robe, she shuffled so slowly and shakily. But she got the robe down and put it on with some difficulty and then proceeded with one foot dragging after the other towards the long table. She stooped, groaning, and straightened up with more creakings and with an enormous book in her arms which she had taken off a shelf beneath the table.

It did not seem likely that she could get far with this additional burden, but she made it, huffing and creaking and even lifted the book above her head to slide it over the front of the tilted-top table. The book slid down until stopped by a strip of wood fixed horizontally halfway up the top. Another strip at the lower edge of the top kept the paper from falling off. He could see that it was a map of the Los Angeles area, just like the maps service stations give to their customers.

His view of it was blocked by the baroness, who climbed back upon the stool, swaying so that he once started to go after her to catch her. She did not fall, and he settled back, asking himself what he cared if she fell. But conditioning took over at the oddest moments, and he had been taught to be kind and respectful to old ladies.

The back of the robe was white with a number of large black

symbols, some of which duplicated those on the wall. The old woman lifted her arms to flap the wide sleeves as if she were an ancient bird about to make a final flight. She began chanting loudly in a foreign tongue which sounded like that used at times by others in the household. Her arms waved; a large gold ring on a finger glinted dully at times, seeming like an eye winking at him.

After a while she stopped chanting and clambered down off the stool again. She tottered to the table and mixed up several of the fluids in the bottles in a glass and drank the contents. She belched loudly; he jumped at its loudness and unexpectedness. She got back on the stool and began to turn the pages of the huge book and, apparently, read a few phrases from each page.

Childe guessed that he was looking upon a genuine magical ritual, genuine in that the witch believed in her magic. What its object was, he did not know. But he felt chilled when he suddenly thought that perhaps she was trying to locate him or influence him by means of this ritual. Not that he believed she could. It was just that he did not like the idea. At another time and under different circumstances, he would have laughed. Too much had happened tonight, however, for him to make light of anything in this house.

Nor did he have any reason to crouch here in the doorway as if waiting to be born. He had to get out, and the only way was past the baroness. There was a door beyond the table; that door, as far as he knew, was the sole exit from the cupola, except for the way by which he had come. That door probably led to a hallway which would lead to a stairway to the lower floors or to a window to the top of a porch.

He doubted that he could get by her without being seen. He would have to knock her out or, if necessary, kill her. There was no reason why he should be gentle. She had to know what was going on here and probably had participated in her younger days or, for all he knew, still did.

Sword in hand, he stood up and walked slowly towards her. Then he stopped. Above her, a very thin haze, greenish-grey, shapeless with some short curling tentacles, had appeared. It could be accounted for if she were smoking. She was not. And the haze grew thicker and spread out sideways and down but not upward.

Childe tried to blink it away. The smoke flowed over her grey Psyche knot of hair and down her neck and over the shoulders of the robe. She was chanting even more loudly and turning the pages of the book more swiftly. She could not be looking up to read the book; her head was bent so far forward that she had to be staring at the map.

Childe felt a little disorientated again. It was as if something were wrong with the world, however, not with him. Then he shook his head and decided to tiptoe by her if he could. She seemed so intent, she might not see him. If the smoke grew thicker, that is, if there indeed *was* smoke and he was not suffering another hallucination, he would be hidden from her.

The smoke did expand and become denser. She was sitting in a ragged column of it. And she was suddenly coughing. Smoke blew out of the way of her breath and then coiled back in to fill the gap. He caught a whiff of a tendril and stepped back. It was acrid, burning, filled with the essence of a million automobile exhausts and smokestack products of chemical factories and refineries.

By now, he was opposite her and could see that the cloud had spread downward and was beginning to cover the map.

She looked up, as if she had suddenly detected his presence. She squalled and fell backward off the stool but whirled and landed on all fours and then was up and running towards the doorway through which he had just come. He was startled for a second at her swiftness and agility but recovered and went after her. She had slammed the door before he could stop her, and when he turned the knob and pulled on it, he found that the door was locked. To break it down was useless, since she would be long gone down the stairway and the passageway.

No, there was Dolores. She might stop the old woman. Then, again, she might not. Her position in this situation was ambiguous. He suspected that her attitude would be what was best for Dolores and that might not coincide with what would be good for him. It would be good sense to quit chasing after the baroness and try to get out before she could warn the others.

The smog over the table was disappearing swiftly and was gone by the time he left the room. The door led directly into an elevator cage which must have been made about 1890. He hated the idea of being trapped in it but he had no other way out. He pressed the DOWN button. Nothing happened except that a small light glowed above the button and a lever near it. He pushed down on the lever, and the elevator began to sink. He pressed more on the lever, and the rate of descent was a little faster. When he pushed the lever upward past the neutral position, the elevator stopped. He pressed the UP button and then pushed the lever upward, and the elevator began to ascend.

Satisfied that he could operate it, he started it downward and stopped at the second storey. If the alarm had been given, they would be waiting for him on the ground floor. They might also be waiting on every floor, but he had to take some chances.

The door was just like the other doors, which was why he may not have known about the elevator. He turned the knob and pushed it and found himself near the door to Magda's bedroom. At the same time, increasingly loud voices and rapid footsteps came up the stairway. He didn't have time to run down the hall and try other doors. He slipped into the room again. Glam's body was still in the marble enclosure, the boots sticking over it. The wall-section was open. He considered for a moment hiding under the many pillows and cushions inside the enclosure but decided that he would be found if they moved Glam's body. There was nothing to do except enter again the passage behind the wall.

He hid behind the inner wall and waited. The first one to step through was going to get a sword in his neck or his guts. The sword trembled in his grip, partly from weariness and partly from nervousness. He had had no experience in swordplay, no fencing lessons, no instructions or conditioned reflexes built up, and so he suddenly realized that he was not as dangerous as he would have liked to be. To handle a sword expertly, a man had to know where to thrust and where not to thrust. An ill-placed stab could hit a bone and glance off and leave the intended victim only lightly wounded and able to run off or attack, if he were tough and experienced. Even a hard musculature could turn an inept thrust.

He swore. He had been so intent on what he was going to do with the sword that he had not noticed that his penis was working up to another orgasm. Stormed, he dropped the sword with a clatter but did not care about the noise for a few seconds. He jetted, the chlorox odour rising strong in the dusty hot passageway. Then he picked up the sword and waited, but he was even more uneasy. Those people out there might have nostrils more sensitive than human beings – he admitted by now that they were not human, as he knew human – and they might easily detect the jism. Should he move on? If so, where? To the same circuit?

He had been running long enough. It was time to fight fire with fire.

Fire.

He looked through the opening. The door of the room was still shut. Loud voices came through it. A savage squeal which chased cold over him. It sounded like an enraged hog. More shouts. Another squeal. The voices seemed to drift away, down the hall. He crept out and inspected the room and found what he wanted. There were books in the shelves, the pages of which he tore out. He crumpled up a *Los Angeles Times* and piled crumpled book-pages over them and ripped open several pillows and sprinkled their contents on the pile. The cigarette lighter in the purse touched off the papers, which soon blazed up and began feeding on the wall-drapes under which the fire had been built.

He opened the door to the hall to open the way for a draught – if it should exist. Taking the classified ad sections of the *Times* and a number of books, he went into the passageway. Having found a one-way mirror, he broke it with the hilt of his sword to make another draught or a reinforcement of the first. He started a fire in the passageway, which was made of old and dry wood and should soon be blazing like the underbrush in the hills at the end of a long dry season. He then entered the room with the broken mirror and built a fire under a huge canopied bed.

Why hadn't he done this before? Because he had been too harried to have time to think, that was why. No more. He was fighting back.

If he could find a room with windows to the outside, he would go through it, even if it meant a drop from the second storey. He'd let them worry about the fire while he got over the walls to his car and back to the police.

He heard voices outside the door to the room and went back into the passageway. He ran down it, using his flashlight, although the fire was providing an adequate twilight for him. A corner took him away from it, however. He stopped and sent the beam down one corridor to check ahead of him. Nothing there. He started to turn to probe the corridor on the other side of the intersection, and he froze. Something had growled at the far end.

Faint clicks sounded. Claws or nails on the naked boards of the floor?

A howl made him jump.

It was a wolf.

Suddenly, the clicking, which had been leisurely, became rapid. The wolf howled again. He turned his flashlight on the corner of the passageway at the far end just in time to see a big grey shape come around it, eyes glowing in the beam. Then the shape, snarling, was

151

bounding towards him.

And behind it came another.

Childe thrust almost blindly at the hurtling shape. His sword travelled in the general direction of the beast as it sprang, but its speed and ferocious voice disconcerted him. Despite this, the blade struck it squarely somewhere. A shock ran along his arm, and, although he had leaned forward in what he hoped was a reasonable imitation of a fencer's lunge, he was thrown backward. He landed on his rump but scrambled to his feet, yelling as he did so. The flashlight, which had fallen, was pointing down along the floor at the second wolf. This was several yards away and crouching as it advanced slowly towards Childe.

It was smaller, the bitch of the pair, and presumably had slowed down to find out what was going on before it attacked.

Childe did not want to expose his side to the bitch, but he did not want to meet her charge without a weapon. He grabbed the hilt of the rapier, put his foot on the body, and pulled savagely. The carcass was palely illuminated in the side-wash of the flashlight. The sword shone dully, and darkness stained the fur around the beast's neck. The rapier had gone in three-quarters of its length, through the neck and out past the bottom rear of the skull.

The rapier pulled out reluctantly but swiftly. The she-wolf snarled and bounded forward, her nails clicking briefly. Childe had a few inches of blade to withdraw yet and would have been taken on the side. Her jaws would probably have clamped on his shoulder or head, and that would have been the end of him. A wolf's jaws were strong enough to sever a man's wrist with one snap.

The bitch, however, slipped on something and skidded on one shoulder into the rump of the dead wolf. Childe leaped backward, taking the sword with him and then as quickly lunged and ran her through the shoulder as she bounded to her feet. She snarled again and her jaws clashed at him, but he pushed with all his weight against the hilt and drove her back so that she fell over the dead wolf. He continued to push, digging his heels into the wood. The blade sank deeper and presently the tip ground against the floor. Before that, the bitch was silent and still.

Shaking, breathing as if his lungs needed oil, he pulled the rapier out and wiped it on the she-wolf's fur. He picked up the flashlight and ran its beam over the wolves to make sure they were dead. Their outlines were becoming indistinct. He felt dizzy and had to shut his eyes and lean against the wall. But he had seen what the bitch had slipped on. A smear of his semen.

Voices drifted around the corner from which the wolves had come. He ran down the passageway, hoping that they would become too occupied with fighting the fires to chase him. The corridor ran into another at right angles to it, and he took the left turn. His beam, dancing ahead of him, picked out a section of wall, and a locking mechanism. He went through it, his sword ready, but he was unable to restrain his wheezing. Any occupant of the room, unless he were deaf, would be warned.

The room was broad and high-ceilinged, so high that it must have displaced two rooms above it and may have gone almost to the roof. The walls were panelled in dark oak, and huge rough-hewn oak beams ran just below the heavily shadowed ceiling. The floor was dark polished oak. Here and there was a wolf or bear skin. The bed was a framework with eight thick rough-hewn oaken logs, low footboard and headboard, and planks laid across the framework.

Lying on the planks was a huge oak log squared off at the corners. It had been gouged out on its top with axe and chisel. The gouge was wide and deep enough to hold a tall man. It did hold a man. The baron, covered with a bearskin to his neck, lay on his back in the hollow. There was dirt beneath him and dirt humped under his head for a pillow.

His face was turned straight upward. His nose looked huge and long. His lower lip had slipped a little to reveal the long white teeth. His face was as greenish-grey as if he had just died. This may have been because of the peculiar greenish light flickering from four fat green candles, two at each corner of the log-coffin.

Childe pulled the bearskin back. The baron was naked. He put his hand on the baron's chest and then on his wrist pulse. There was no detectable heartbeat, and the chest did not move. An eyelid, peeled back, showed only white.

Childe left the baron and pulled two drapes back. Two enormous french windows were greyly bared. It was daytime, but the light was very dark, as if night had left an indelible stain. The sky was dark grey with streamers of green-grey dangling here and there.

Childe looked in the darkness under the planks supporting the log-coffin. He found a roughly-worked oaken lid. He felt cold. The silence, the sputtering green candles, the heavy dark wood everywhere, the ponderous beams, which seemed to drip shadows, the roughness, indeed, the archaicness, of the room, and the corpse-like sleeper, who was so expected and yet so unexpected – these fell like heavy shrouds, one over the other, upon him. His breath sawed in his throat.

Was this room supposed to be a reproduction of a room in the ancestral castle in the Carpathians? Why the ubiquitous primitively worked oak? And why this coffin when Igescu could afford the best?

Some things here accorded with the superstitions (which, as far as he was concerned, were not superstitions). Other things he could not account for.

He had a hunch that this room was built to conform to specifications far more ancient than medieval ones, that the oak and the log and the candles had been in use long before the Carpathian mountains were so named, long before Rumania existed as a colony of the Romans, long before the mother city, Rome, existed, and probably long before the primitive Indo-European speakers began to spread out of the homeland of what would someday be called Austria and Hungary. A type of this room, and a type of this man who slept in the log, in one form or another, had existed in central Europe, and elsewhere, when men spoke languages now perished without a record and when they still used flint tools.

Whatever the origin of his kind, however closely or distantly he resembled the creature of folklore, legend, and superstition, Igescu was forced to be as good as dead when daylight arrived. The rays of the sun contained some force responsible for diurnal suspended animation. Perhaps some other phenomenon connected with the impact of the sun caused this strange sleep. Or, perhaps, it was the other way around, with the absence of the moon? No, that wasn't logical because the moon was often present in the daytime. But then, maybe the moon's effect was greatly reduced by the other luminary.

If Igescu had not been forced to do so, he would never have quit the search for Dolores and Childe. Why, then, had he not made sure that he would not be vulnerable? He knew that both Dolores and Childe were in the intramural passageways.

Childe felt colder than before except for a hot spot between his shoulder blades, the focus of something hidden somewhere and staring at his back.

He looked swiftly around the room, at the ceiling, where the shadows clung above the beams, under the oaken frame of the bed, although he had looked there once, and behind the few chairs. There was nothing.

The bathroom was empty. So was the room beyond the thick rough oaken door on the west wall. Nothing living was there but a massive mahogany coffin with gold trimming and gold-plated handles stood in one corner.

Childe raised the lid, fully expecting to find a body. It was empty. Either it had housed a daylight sleeper at one time or it was to be used in some emergency by the baron. Childe pulled up the satin lining and found earth beneath it.

He went back to the oaken room. Nothing had visibly changed. Yet the silence seemed to creak. It was as if intrusion of another had hauled in the slack of the atmosphere, had hauled it in too tightly. The shadows abruptly seemed darker; the green light of the candles was heavier and, in some way, even more sinister.

He stood in the doorway, sword ready, motionless, repressing his breathing so he could listen better.

Something had come into this room, either from the passageway entrance or through the door at the west wall. He doubted that it had used the passageway entrance, because any guard stationed there would have challenged him before he could get into the room.

It had to have been in the other room, and it must have been watching him through some aperture, which Childe could not discern. It had not moved against him immediately because he had not tried to harm the baron.

Perhaps the feeling was only too-strained nerves. He could see nothing, nothing at all to alarm him.

But the baron would not have left himself unguarded.

19

Childe took one step forward. There was still no sound except that which his mental ear heard. It was a crackling, as if the intrusion of a new mass had bent a magnetic field. The lines of force had been pushed out.

The rapier held point up, he advanced towards the enormous log on the bed. The noiseless crackling became louder. He stooped and looked under the frame. There was nothing there.

Something heavy struck him on his back and drove him face down. He screamed and rolled over. Fire tore at his back and his hips and the back of his thighs, but he was up and away, while something snarled and spat behind him. He rounded the bed and whirled, the sword still in his hand although he had no memory of consciously clinging to it or of even thinking of it. But if his spirit had unclenched for a moment, his fist had not.

The thing was a beauty and terror of white and black rosetted fur, and taut yellow-green eyes which seemed to reflect the ghastly light of the candles, and thin black lips, and sharp yellow teeth. It was small for a leopard but large enough to scare him even after most of the fright of the unexpected and unknown had left him. It had hidden in the cavity of the log, crouching flattened on top of Igescu until Childe had come close enough for it.

Now it crouched again and snarled, eyes spurting ferocity, claws unsheathed.

Now it launched itself over the bed and the coffin. Childe, leaning over the baron's body, thrust outward. The cat was spitted on the blade, which drove through the neck. A paw flashed before his eyes, but the tips of the claws were not quite close enough. Childe went over backward, and the rapier was torn from his hand. When he got up, he saw that the leopard, a female, was kicking its last. It lay on its right side, mouth open, the life in its eyes flying away bit by bit, like a flock of bright birds leaving a branch one by one as they started south to avoid the coming of winter.

Childe was panting and shaking, and his heart was threatening to butt through his ribs. He pulled the sword out, shoving with his foot against the body, and then climbed upon the oaken frame. He raised the sword before him by the hilt with both hands. Its point was downward, parallel with his body. He held it as if he were a monk holding a cross up to ward off evil which, in a way, he was. He brought the blade down savagely with all his weight and drove it through the skin and heart and, judging from the resistance and muted cracking sound, some bones.

The body moved with the impact, and the head turned a little to one side. That was all. There was no sighing or rattling of breath. No blood spurted from around the wound or even seeped out.

The instrument of execution was steel, not wood, but the hilt formed a cross. He hoped that the symbol was more important than the material. Perhaps neither meant anything. It might be mistaken lore which said that a vampire, to be truly killed, must be pierced through the heart with a stake or that the undead feared the cross with an unholy dread and were deprived of force in its presence.

Also, he remembered from his reading of *Dracula*, many years ago, something about the head having to be removed.

He felt that probably there were many things said about this creature that were not true and also there were many things unknown. Whether the lore was superstition or not, he had done his best, was going to do his best, to ensure that it died a permanent death.

As for the leopard, it might be just that – a leopard. He suspected that it was Ngima or Mrs Pocyotl because it was so small. It did not seem likely that Pocyotl, who was Mexican, some of whose ancestors undoubtedly spoke one form or another of Nahuatl, would be a wereleopard. A werejaguar, yes. No, it must be, if not a genuine leopard, Ngima or the Chinaman Pao.

Whatever it was, it showed so sign of changing after death. Perhaps it really was not a metamorph, but a pet trained to guard Igescu.

What am I thinking of? he thought. Of course, it is. There are no such creatures as werewolves and wereleopards and vampires. Maybe there are vampires, psychological vampires, psychotics who think they are vampires. But an actual metamorphosis! What kind of mechanism would be involved, what mechanism could affect a change like that? Bones become fluid, change shape even in the cellular structure, and harden again? Well, maybe the bones are not *our* kind of bones. But what about the energy involved? And even if the body could shift shape, the brain surely couldn't! The brain would have to retain its human size and shape.

He looked at the leopard and he remembered the wolves. Their heads were wolf-sized, their brains were small.

He should forget this nonsense. He had been drugged; the rest was suggestion.

Not until then did he become aware that the leopard, when it had been fastened to him for such a short time, had done more than he had thought. It had torn off his shirt and pants and belt, and his hand, feeling his back and hips and legs, was wet with blood. He hurt, and he was alarmed, but a closer examination convinced him that the leopard had done more harm to his clothes than to him. The wounds were superficial or seemed so.

He went into the next room, which was a small study, and picked up an armful of newspapers and magazines. Returning to the huge room, he wadded up the papers and ripped out pages and stacked a pile on each side of the baron's neck. After dripping some lighter fluid on the two piles and over the baron's hair and chest, he touched off the fluid.

Childe then opened the large windows and built another fire below the central plank. A third pile below the left side of the framework blazed up. In a few minutes, he added a wooden chair to that fire. After a while, the oak of the frame and the plank were blazing, and the log was blackening and smoking. The stench of burned hair and flesh rose from the baron.

More paper and lighter fluid got the drapes over the windows to burning. Then he struggled with the body of the leopard until he had dropped it on the fire. Its head burned fiercely with lighter fluid; its black nose lost its wet shininess and wrinkled with heat.

Opening the entrance to the passageway made a stronger draught. The smoke in the room streamed out through the hole to meet the smoke in the passageway.

The entrance did not seem big enough to handle all the smoke, which soon filled the room. He began to cough and, suddenly, as if the coughs had triggered him, he had a long shuddering orgasm the roots of which seemed to be wrapped around his spine and to be pulling his spine down his back and out through his penis.

Just as the last spurt came, a shriek tore from the smoke in the centre of the room. He spun around but could see nothing. One of the two had not been dead and still was not dead because the shrieks were continuing with full strength.

And then, before he could turn again to face the new sound, a grunting and squealing shot from the wall-entrance. There was a rapid clicking, much louder than the wolves' claws, a tremble of the boards under his feet and he was knocked upward to one side. Half-stunned, his left leg hurting, he sat up. He began coughing. The squealing became louder and the boards shook under him. He rolled away under cover of the smoke, while the thing that had hit him charged around, hunting for him.

Crawling on his hands and knees along the wall, his head bent near the floor to keep from breathing the smoke, he headed for the french windows. The swine noises had now given way to a deep coughing. After a dozen racks that seemed strong enough to suck in all the smoke in the room during the in-breaths, the hooves clattered again. Childe rounded the corner and slid along the wall until he came to the next corner. His hand, groping upward into the smoke, felt the lower edges of the french windows. The open ones were about ten feet away, as he remembered them.

The hooves abruptly stopped. The squealing was even more ferocious, less questing and more challenging. Hooves hit the floorboards again. Punctuating the two sounds was a loud hissing.

A battle was taking place somewhere in the smoke. Several times, the walls shook as heavy bodies hit them, and the floor seldom ceased to tremble. Blows – a great hand hammering into a thick solid body – added codas to the crackling of the fires.

Childe could not have waited to see what was going on even if he had wished. The smoke would kill him sooner, the fire would kill him later, but not so much later, if he did not get out. There was no time to crawl on around until he got to the west door. The windows were the only way out. He climbed out after unfastening and pushing out the lower edge of the screen, let himself down until he clung by his hands, and then dropped. He struck a bush, broke it, felt as if he had broken himself, too, rolled off it and then stood up. His left leg hurt even more, but he could see no blood.

And then he jetted again – at least, his penis had not been hurt in the fall – and was helpless while two bodies hurtled through the window he had just left. The screen, torn off, struck near him. Magda Holyani and Mrs Grasatchow crushed more bushes and rolled off them on to the ground near the driveway.

Immediately after, several people ran out of the house on to the porch.

Both the women were bleeding from many wounds and blackened with smoke. Magda had ended her roll at his feet in time to receive a few drops on her forehead. This, he could not help thinking even in his pain, was an appropriate extreme unction for her. The fat woman had struck as heavily as a sack of wet flour and now lay unconscious, a grey bone sticking out of the flesh of one leg and blood running from her ears and nostrils.

Bending Grass, Mrs Pocyotl, and O'Faithair were on the porch. That left Chornkin, Krautschner, Ngima, Pao, Vivienne, the two maids, the baroness, and Dolores unaccounted for. He thought he knew what had happened to the first three. Two were dead of rapier thrusts in a passageway and one was burning with Igescu.

The clothes of the three on the porch were ripped, their hair was disarrayed, and they were bleeding from wounds. They must have tangled with Magda or Mrs Grasatchow or Dolores or any combination thereof. But they were not disabled, and they were now looking for him, their mouths moving, their hands moving to indicate him now and then.

Childe limped, but swiftly, to the Rolls-Royce parked twenty feet away on the driveway. Behind came a shout and shoes slapping against the porchsteps. The Rolls was unlocked, and the key was in the ignition lock. He drove away while Bending Grass and O'Faithair beat on the windows with their fists and howled like wolves at him. Then they had dropped off and were racing towards another car, a red Jaguar.

Childe stopped the Rolls, reversed, and pressed the accelerator to the floor. Going backward, the Rolls bounced O'Faithair off the right rear fender and then crashed to a halt. Bending Grass had whirled just before it pinned him against the Jaguar. His dark broad face stared into the rear window for a few seconds. Then it was gone.

Childe drove forward until he could see the Indian's body, red and mashed from the thighs down, face downward on the pavement. The outlines of his body looked fuzzy; he seemed to be swelling.

Childe had no time to keep looking. He stopped the Rolls again, backed it up over O'Faithair, who was just beginning to sit up, went forward over him again, turned around, and drove the wheels back and forth three times each over the bodies of Holyani, Grasatchow, Bending Grass, and O'Faithair. Mrs Pocyotl, who had been screaming at him and shaking her little fist, ran back into the house when he drove towards the porch.

Flames and smoke were pouring out of a dozen windows on all three storeys of the left wing and out of one window of the central

160

house. Unchecked, the first would destroy the entire building in an hour or two. And there was nobody to check it.

He drove away. Coming around the curve just before entering the road through the woods, he saw part of the yard to one side of the house. The red-headed Vivienne, her naked body white in the ghastly half-dark daylight, Mrs Pocyotl with her shoes off, and the two maids were running for the woods. Behind them came the nude Dolores, her long dark hair flying. She looked grim and determined. The others looked determined also, but their determination was inspired by fright.

Childe did not know what she would do if she caught them, but he was sure that they knew and were not standing to fight for good reasons. He also suspected that Pao and the baroness had not come out of the house because of what Dolores had done to them, although it was possible that Magda or Mrs Grasatchow had killed them. He could not be sure, of course, but he suspected that the two had been in metamorphosis as pig and snake and that they had been unmanageable.

The three women disappeared in the trees.

He struck himself on the forehead. Was he really believing all this metamorphosis nonsense?

He looked back. From this slight rise, he could see Bending Grass and Mrs Grasatchow. The clothes seemed to have split off the Indian, and he looked black and bulky, like a bear. The fat woman was also dark and there was something non-human about the corpse.

At that moment, from behind the house, the biggest black fox he had ever seen raced out and tore off towards the woods into which the three women had disappeared. It barked three times and then turned its head and seemed to grin at him.

The chill that had transfixed him when he first saw Dolores went through him again. He remembered something now, something he had read long ago. The shape-shifting fox-people of China. They lost control of their ability to change form if they drank too much wine. And, that first evening, the baron had been trying to restrain Pao's wine consumption. Why? Because he had not wanted Childe to witness the metamorphosis? Or for some other reason? For some other reason, probably, since the baron could not have been worried about Childe escaping to tell what he had seen.

He shrugged and drove on. He had had too much of this and wanted only to get away. He was beginning to believe that a 150 pound man

161

could become fluid, twist bone and flesh into a nonhuman mould, and, somewhere along the transformation, shed 125 pounds, just tuck them away some place to be withdrawn later when needed. Or, if not cached, the discarded mass trailed along, like an invisible jet exhaust, an attached plume of energy ready for reconversion.

The gate of the inner wall was before him. He opened this and drove through, and soon was stopped by the outer wall. Here he left the Rolls on the driveway, after wiping off his prints with a rag from the glove compartment, and walked through the big gate to his own car, parked under the trees at the end of the road.

He found the key he had hidden – how long ago? it seemed days – and drove away. He was naked, bloody, bruised, and hurting, and he still had an erection that was automatically working up to yet another – oh, God! – orgasm, but he did not care. He would get into his apartment, and the rest of the world, smog, monsters, and all, could go to hell, which they were doing, anyway.

A half-mile down the road, a big black Lincoln shot by him towards the Igescu estate. It held three men and three women, all of whom were handsome or beautiful and well dressed. Their faces were, however, grim, and he knew that their destination was Igescu's and that they were speeding because they were late for whatever sinister conference they had been scheduled to attend. Or because someone in the house had called them for help. The car had California licence plates. Perhaps they were from San Francisco.

He smiled feebly. They would be unpleasantly surprised. Meanwhile, he had better get out of here, because he did not know whether or not they had noted his licence plate.

Before he had gone a mile, the sky had become even darker, growled, thundered, lightninged. A strong wind tore the smog apart, and then the rains washed the air and the earth without let-up for an hour and a half.

He parked the car in the underground garage and took the elevator up to his floor. No one saw him, although he expected to be observed. He had no excuse for being naked and with a hard-on, and it would be just like life, the great ironist, to have him arrested for indecent exposure and God knows what else after all he had been through, he, the abused innocent. But no one saw him, and, after locking the door and chaining it, he showered, dried himself, put on pyjamas, ate a ham and cheese sandwich and drank half a quart of milk, and crawled into bed.

162

Just before he fell asleep, a few seconds later, he put out his hand to feel for something. What did he want? Then he realized that it was Mrs Grasatchow's purse, which contained the skins. Somewhere between the baron's bedroom and this bedroom, he had lost the purse.

Childe slept, though often restlessly, for a day, a night, and most of the next day. He got up to empty bladder and bowels, to eat cereal or a sandwich and sometimes woke up at the end of a wet dream.

His dreams were often terrors, but were sometimes quite pleasant copulations. Sometimes Mrs Grasatchow or Vivienne or Dolores rode him, and he woke up jetting and groaning. Other times, he was riding Sybil or some woman he had known or some faceless woman. And there were at least two dreams in which he was mounting a female animal from the rear, once with a beautiful leopardess and once with a bitch wolf.

When he was awake, he wondered about the dreams, because he knew that the Freudians insisted that all dreams, no matter how terrifying or horrible, were wishes.

By the time he was slept out, pyjamas and sheets were a mess, but the effects of the cone were gone. He was very happy to have a flaccid penis. He showered and breakfasted, and then read the latest *Los Angeles Times*. Life was almost normal now; the papers were being delivered on schedule. Industries were running full-time. The migration back was still going on but was only a trickle now. The mortuaries were overloaded, and funerals were taking place far into the night. The police were swamped with missing persons reports. Otherwise, the city was functioning as usual. The smog was beginning to build up but would not become alarming while the present breeze continued.

Childe read the front page and some articles. Then he used the phone to check on Sybil. She had not come home. A call to San Francisco was answered by Sybil's sister, Cherril. She said that the mother had died, and Sybil was supposed to have come for the funeral. She presumably left as soon as she had packed. She had been unable to get a plane out, and her car wouldn't start, so she had phoned back that she was coming up with a friend who also wanted to get out of town.

Who was the friend? Cherril did not know. But she was frantic, and she had tried to get hold of Childe. When he had not answered after five tries, she had given up on him. The state police had reported that Sybil was not involved in any of the many accidents between Los

Angeles and San Francisco during that time.

Childe told Cherril not to worry, that many people were still missing. Sybil would show up safe and sound. He would not rest until he found her. And so on.

When he hung up the phone, he felt empty. The next day, he was as hollow, and he had to admit that he knew no more than what Cherril had told him. The 'friend' he suspected Sybil to have driven off with, Al Porthouse, denied having seen her for two weeks.

Childe gave up, temporarily, and turned his attention elsewhere. The baron's house had been burned out, although the rains had kept it from being completely destroyed. There were no bodies in the ruins, in the yard, or in the woods. Mrs Grasatchow's purse was not found.

Childe remembered the automobile that had raced by him after he had driven away from the baron's. Whoever the six had been, they had cleaned up thoroughly.

But what had happened to Dolores?

He drove out to the estate and went over the wall again, the police having locked the main gate. His poking around uncovered nothing. The police did not know his story, of course. He knew better than to tell them anything except that he had visited the baron just once and that briefly. They had questioned him and then had said that they were puzzled by the disappearance of the baron, secretary, servants, and chauffeur, but so far no information had come in. For all they knew, the household had left for parts unknown, the house had burned by accident, and any day now they might hear from the baron.

Late that afternoon, he returned to his apartment. He was shrouded in his thoughts, which were concerned with moving elsewhere, to some place where smog would not be a problem for years to come. It was some time before he realized that the phone must have rung at least a dozen times. It had started while he was unlocking the door.

The voice was a pleasant baritone.

'Mr Childe? You don't know me. We haven't met, fortunately for you, although I think we passed each other on the road outside the Baron Igescu's estate several days ago.'

Childe did not reply for a moment, then he said, 'What do you want?'

His voice was steady. He had thought it would crack, as if it were

165

crystallized with the ice encasing him.

'You have been very discreet, Mr Childe, in not telling the police. Or as far as we know, anybody. But we want to ensure your silence, Mr Childe. We could easily do that by methods you well know by now. But it pleases us to have you know about us and yet be able to do nothing.'

Childe shouted, 'What did you do with Sybil?'

There was a silence. And then the voice, 'Sybil? Who's she?'

'My wife! My ex-wife, I mean! You know, damn you! What have you done with her, you filthy monster, unnatural . . !'

'Nothing, I assure you, Mr Childe.'

The voice was cool and mocking.

'We rather admire you, Mr Childe, because of what you accomplished. Congratulations. You managed to kill, permanently, a number of our friends who have survived for a very long time indeed, Mr Childe. You could not have done it without the help of del Osorojo, of course, but that was something we did not foresee. The baron did not anticipate it, and for his carelessness, or ignorance, he paid, and those with him. Some of them, anyway.'

This was his last chance to find out anything about them.

He said, 'Why the films? Why were they sent in to the police?'

'The films are made for our private use, for our entertainment, Mister Childe. We send them to each other all over the world. Via private couriers, of course. The baron decided to break a precedent and to let the *others* in on some of them. Because we would enjoy the furore and the shaking up of the police. The shaking up of all humans, in fact. The baron and his group were going to move out soon, anyway, so there was no chance of our being connected with the films.

'The baron planned on mailing the films of earlier subjects, working backward chronologically, to the police. Most of the subjects had been listed as missing persons, you know, and the earliest had been dropped by the police because the cases were so old. You found their skins. And lost them.

'You were lucky or smart. You used an unorthodox method of investigation and stumbled across the truth. The baron couldn't let you go then because you knew too much, so he decided you would become the latest subject. Now, the baron won't have to leave this area to get away from the smog . . '

'I saw the old woman, the baroness, trying to conjure up smog!'

166

Childe said. 'What . . '

'She was trying to get rid of it, you fool! This used to be a nice place to live in, but you humans . . !'

Childe could feel the fury making the man inarticulate. However, when the voice returned, it was again cool and mocking.

'I suggest you look in your bedroom. And remember to keep silent, Mister Childe. Otherwise . . .'

The phone must have been travelling down to the rest. But, before the click, he heard bells tolling, and an organ playing the first bar of *Gloomy Sunday*. He could imagine the rest of the music and the Inner-Sanctum rusty-hinge screeching.

He stood for a while with the phone in his hand. Woolston Heepish? That call came from the house of Woolston Heepish?

Nonsense! There must be another explanation. He did not even want to think about the implications, if . . . no, forget this.

He put the phone down, and then remembered with a start what the man had advised. He slowly walked into the bedroom. The bedside lamp had been turned on during his absence.

She was in bed, staring straight up. A sheet was draped over her to just below the naked breasts. Her black hair was spread out on the pillow.

He came closer and murmured, 'I didn't think they could harm you, Dolores.'

He pulled the sheet back, expecting to find the evidences of some horror committed upon her. She was unmarked.

But her body tilted upward, the feet rising first, the stiff legs following, and then, as the body began to point straight upward, it rose towards the ceiling. The heavy hair, and the little red valve on the back of the neck, stopped it from floating up all the way.

The make-up was very good. It had given her skin a solid fleshy appearance and kept him from seeing through it.

Childe had to leave the room for a while and sit down.

When he came back, he stuck a pin in her. She exploded with a bang as loud as a pistol's. He cut her up into strips with scissors and flushed her down the toilet, except for the head of hair, which he put into the garbage.

A century and a half of haunting, a brief fleshing, a few short and wild copulations, a few killings of ancient enemies, and here she was. Rather, there she went. One dark eye, long eyelashes, a thick eyebrow whirled around and then were sucked down.

At least, he had not found Sybil's skin in his bed.

Where was she? He might never find out. He did not think those 'people' knew. The 'man' had sounded genuinely puzzled.

It was not necessary to postulate those 'people' to account for her disappearance. Human beings had enough monsters of their own.

Postscript

'So you're writing pornography now?' Thus spake one of the acquaintances of Philip José Farmer recently. The question seems simple and straightforward. It was, obviously, asked by a man who honestly felt he could define his own terms, and probably that the terms he used were so self-evident that they didn't need defining.

There is a vast number of honestly simple-minded people who can, without hesitation, define

pornography	science fiction
God	communism
right	freedom
evil	honourable peace
liberty	obscenity
law and order	love

and think, and act, and legislate, and sometimes burn, jail, and kill on the basis of their definitions. These are the Labellers, and they are without exception the most lethal and destructive force ever faced by any species of this or any other planet, and I shall tell you clearly and simply why.

Simply truth is hard to come by. Virtually everything which looks like the truth is subject to question and modification. 'Water runs downhill.' At what temperature? Where – in an Apollo capsule, for example, or in the input end of a siphon? 'Skirts are for girls.' Would you like to face up to a battalion of the kilted Black Watch or a company of the hard-bitten Greek *evzones*? (They even have lace on their skirts.) '$E=MC^2$', said that burnished deity of the relative, Albert Einstein, 'may after all be a local phenomenon.'

The lethal destructiveness inherent in Labelling lies in the fact that the Labeller, without exception, overlooks the most basic of all characteristics of everything in the universe – *passage*: that is to say, flux and change. If he stops and thinks (which is not his habit) the Labeller must concede that rocks change, and mountains; that the planets change, and the stars, and that they have not stopped because of the purely local and most minor phenomenon that he happens to be placing a Label in this place at this point in time.

Passage is more evident in what we call life than in any other area. It is not enough to say that living things change; one must go further and say that life *is* change. That which does not change is abhorrent to the most basic laws of the universe; that which does not change is not alive; and in the presence of that which does not change, life cannot exist.

That is why the Labeller is lethal. He is the dead hand. His is the command, *Stop!* He is death's friend, life's enemy. He does not want, he cannot face, things as they really are ... moving, flowing, changing; he wants them to stop.

Why?

I think it's because of a perfectly normal desire for security. He wants to feel safe. He does not know that he has mistaken stasis for stability. If only everything would stop; if only today and tomorrow would be just like yesterday (he never looks carefully at yesterday, you understand, so he thinks everything was motionless and peaceful and law-abiding yesterday, which of course it wasn't) he could really feel safe. He doesn't realize that he has become anti-life and pro-death – that what he is actually about is a form of suicide, for himself and his species. He doesn't realize that in the sanctuary of the church of his choice, any given Sunday (or Saturday) morning, he will see respectable matrons dressed in clothes which would have been forbidden, not only on the streets, but on the beaches, within the memory of the older parishioners. He has forgotten that it was only a few short years ago that something close to cultural shock swept through our species because Clark Gable, as Rhett Butler, said 'Damn' in a movie. He overlooks all evidence, all truth, and he Labels; and he is absolutely deadly, so watch out for him.

Philip José Farmer is a superb writer and in every sense a good man, who seems to have been born with the knowledge that the truth – the real truth – is to be sought with the devotion of those who sought the Holy Grail, and to be faced openly, even when it turned out to be something that he and the rest of us would much rather it wasn't. Ever since (in 1952) he exploded into science fiction with an extraordinary novelette called *The Lovers*, he has continued to call it what it is, show it as he finds it. The book you hold in your hands is a perfect case in point. The Labellers will be gone from here long about Page 2, crying 'Stop!' (A word which of all words is most against God.) A handful of poor tilted souls, whom the Labellers have frustrated and perverted, will drool wetly all the way through, skipping all the living connective tissue and getting their jollies out of

170

context. (Some of these will thereafter destructively Label the book, to Stop anyone else from getting any.) The rest of you will take these pages for what they are: truths (for many of these things are truly within us all, whether you find that a pleasant truth or not) and the seeking for truth; the symbols and analogues of truth and of the quest for truth – and a hell of a good story.

After I had read *The Image of the Beast*, and before I wrote these comments, I called Phil Farmer for one clarification. In all my reading and researching, and in all my hardly impoverished imaginings, I had *never* run across an image like the one concerning 'the most beautiful woman in the world' and the long, glistening thing, with a golf-ball-sized head complete with a face and a little beard, which emerged from her womb and entered her throat. Aside from the amazement and shock which it evokes, it filled me with wonder, for it is unique, and was, to me, without literary or psychopathological referents. They are, he tells me, Joan of Arc and the famous/infamous Gilles de Rais (which in itself is an odd coupling!), and he went on to tell me that they are part of a far larger symbolic structure, to be elucidated in two more books. This is why *Image* has the subtitle-note *An exorcism: Ritual 1*. Therefore, like everything else Farmer has written, *Image* is fable. That is to say, like all of Aesop and a lot of Shakespeare, the story is larger than the narrative – the play means more than the events described. Calculated discomfort is a well-known path to truth. The lotus position is at first an agony. A fast of forty days and nights is only for the dedicated, and while it might lead to a meeting with Satan, it is recorded somewhere that Satan can thereupon be defeated. I take Farmer's structured shock accordingly, and go with it, and eagerly await the completion of his pattern.

For you can't keep a good man down, friends and Labellers – neither his goodness nor his manhood.

– Theodore Sturgeon

The world's greatest science fiction authors
now available in Panther Books

Philip José Farmer
The Riverworld Saga

To Your Scattered Bodies Go	£1.25	☐
The Fabulous Riverboat	£1.50	☐
The Dark Design	£1.95	☐
The Magic Labyrinth	£1.95	☐

Other Titles

Dark is the Sun	£1.95	☐
Jesus on Mars	£1.50	☐
Riverworld and other stories	£1.50	☐
The Stone God Awakens	£1.50	☐
Time's Last Gift	£1.50	☐
Traitor to the Living	85p	☐
Strange Relations	£1.25	☐
The Unreasoning Mask	£1.95	☐
The Book of Philip José Farmer	£1.95	☐

To order direct from the publisher just tick the titles you want
and fill in the order form.   SF281

The world's greatest science fiction authors now available in Panther Books

To order direct from the publisher just tick the titles you want and fill in the order form.

SF481

The world's greatest science fiction authors now available in Panther Books

Robert Silverberg

Earth's Other Shadow	£1.50	☐
The World Inside	£1.50	☐
Tower of Glass	£1.50	☐
Recalled to Life	£1.50	☐
Invaders from Earth	£1.50	☐
Master of Life and Death	£1.50	☐

J G Ballard

The Crystal World	75p	☐
The Drought	£1.50	☐
Hello America	£1.50	☐
The Disaster Area	£1.50	☐
Crash	£1.50	☐
Low-Flying Aircraft	75p	☐
The Atrocity Exhibition	£1.50	☐
The Venus Hunters	£1.50	☐
The Unlimited Dream Company	£1.25	☐
Concrete Island	60p	☐

Philip Mann

The Eye of the Queen	£1.95	☐

To order direct from the publisher just tick the titles you want
and fill in the order form.

SF581

All these books are available at your local bookshop or newsagent, or can be ordered direct from the publisher..

To order direct from the publisher just tick the titles you want and fill in the form below.

Name _____

Address _____

_____

Send to:
Panther Cash Sales
PO Box 11, Falmouth, Cornwall TR10 9EN.

Please enclose remittance to the value of the cover price plus:

UK 45p for the first book, 20p for the second book plus 14p per copy for each additional book ordered to a maximum charge of £1.63.

BFPO and Eire 45p for the first book, 20p for the second book plus 14p per copy for the next 7 books, thereafter 8p per book.

Overseas 75p for the first book and 21p for each additional book.

Panther Books reserve the right to show new retail prices on covers, which may differ from those previously advertised in the text or elsewhere.